Howard Pease

Borderland Studies

Howard Pease

Borderland Studies

ISBN/EAN: 9783337335984

Printed in Europe, USA, Canada, Australia, Japan

Cover: Foto ©Andreas Hilbeck / pixelio.de

More available books at **www.hansebooks.com**

BORDERLAND STUDIES.

BORDERLAND STUDIES.

BY

HOWARD PEASE.

—

"The Hotspur of the North; he that kills me some six or seven
dozen of Scots at a breakfast, washes his hands, and says to his wife:
'Fie upon this quiet life! I want work.'"—*1st Part King Henry IV.*

"Fain would I be in the North Countrie,
There would I see what is pleasant to me."
—*Old Northumbrian Ballad.*

NEWCASTLE-ON-TYNE:

MAWSON, SWAN, & MORGAN.

LONDON:

SIMPKIN, MARSHALL, HAMILTON, KENT, & Co., LTD.

—

1893.

TO

C. L. Graves,

PREFACE.

OF the following Sketches, "Children of Boreas" and "Upon the Advantage of being a Scot," appeared in Mr. Greenwood's *Anti-Jacobin*, "Our Village," and "With the North Countrie Methodies," in the *National Observer*, while of the Tales, "The Elder of North Quay" is but the "second name," to use an old Quaker term, of "The Pearl of Hafiz," which appeared in the pages of the *Gentleman's Magazine*. The Author here desires to express his thanks to the editors of the above periodicals for their courteous permission to reprint these articles. The remainder of the volume consists of fresh matter.

And now, lest the reader should shrewdly suspect the Author of endeavouring, under a specious title, to fobb off, like the tricksy auctioneer, an "odd lot" of articles upon his credulity, a few words may perhaps be permitted concerning the Genesis of the book.

Finding that the above-mentioned sketches had met with some approbation, it occurred to the Author to increase their number and to add thereto a like quantity of Tales, which should illustrate the characteristics of the North Countrie Folk, previously dealt with realistically, in romantic or idealistic fashion, for he believed that the hard and resolute, rugged and tenacious character of the race was well adapted to this purpose, and at the same time he conceived the project to possess some degree of novelty. The ancient temper of the country—that *perfervidum ingenium*—to which the Northumbrian, equally with the Scot, may lay claim, though it may have changed its direction, still survives to this present with unabated force.

As formerly he was amongst the last energetically to support the *jus divinum* of the Stuarts, so now he is amongst the first as keenly to uphold the modern theory of the *jus divinum* of the working man. When Mr. Anthony Hillyard (in Mr. Besant's novel, "Dorothy Forster") discussed the prospects of the premeditated Jacobite rising in the '15, he was ever anxious to enquire how the City of London was minded on the matter, considering all attempt hopeless if the city were averse from their cause.

Somewhat similarly the writer well remembers when at Oxford how his tutor used ever to ask, when discussing the latest industrial problem or socialistic theory : What Tyneside thought upon the question ?—plainly intimating that what Tyneside thought to-day the progressive part of the community elsewhere would generally accept to-morrow.

In conclusion the writer would apologise for what has been called by a friendly critic, " the sombre colouring " of the tales, pointing out, however, in self defence, that Northumbria is no Phæacia, no land of soft delights where always

$$\Delta aίς \; τε \; φίλη \; Κίθαρίς \; τε \; Χοροί \; τε$$
$$εἵματα \; ἐξημοιβὰ \; λοετρὰ \; τε \; Θερμὰ \; καί \; εὐναί.$$

but a bleak and wind-bitten northern region, where life is hard, and men's thoughts and deeds, as a consequence, are something grim in their inclination.

ARCOT HALL,
    DUDLEY,
        NORTHUMBERLAND.

SKETCHES.

THE BORDERLAND.

THE stranger, whirling rapidly Northward through
Northumberland by the East Coast service of trains,
may catch an occasional glimpse of mighty castles by the
sea, or again, preferring the more leisurely route, thoughtfully provided by the North British Railway Company for
the better appreciation of the landscape, he may see, ere
he cross the Border, full many a ruined peel tower and
ancient stronghold, and many an unmistakable evidence,
if he have the antiquary's eye, of the stormy life of olden
time.

Camp and barrow, cairn and tower, quaint-named fell
and haugh are all so many proofs of a tumultuous past,
each a link in the self-same stirring tale which crenellated
mansion, hidden monastery, and sea-girt castle continue
and carry forward to a later age.

Before the traveller's eye, as he faces westward towards
the Border, the naked fells of the " terra contentiosa "—
that debatable land of old, will open out, rolling away as
on a full tide, to a high horizon, desolate as a November
sea.

Often, save for the scattered sheep, no sign of life is
visible, and, save for the cry of the curlew, no sound
is audible. In the lonely clumps of firs that here and
there crown the grey-green grassy slopes, fancy may
picture a plump of Border spears hard-spurring towards
the haugh below to carry off the sheep and " nowt." It
may be a troop from Liddesdale, or it may be a company
of Robsons eager to harry the Grahams once again, and
hang the chiefest among their number as a warning, that
" the neist tyme gentlemen cam to tak their schepe, they
war no to be scabbit." Here, indeed, the mind may gallop
to imagination's prick, for the past, like an open page, is
spread before the eye ; and not alone is the face of Nature

unchanged, for the very dwellers in the dales bear the names of the " graynes " of old.

Writing so lately as 1871, Dr. Charlton relates that famous " Muckle Jock " of Bellingham remembered more than once clearing Bellingham Fair with the Tarset and Tarretburn men at his back to the ancient Border cry—

> " Tarset and Tarretburn
> Hard and heather-bred
> Yet, yet, yet."

To this day, indeed, about Bellingham, at a fair or football match, may the " Yet, yet, yet," of the old Border slogan be heard.

The ancient feuds, too, between the various dalesmen have only recently been extinguished, stray embers, even within living memory, having been momentarily blown into heat upon occasion, as when at Harbottle Fair in Coquetdale, some fifty years ago, a Redesdale man was heard disconsolately to remark, " Aw nivor seed sic a fair i' maa life, past 'leven o'clock o' the forenoon an' nivor a broken heid."

The writer himself has heard, high up in Coquetdale, upon an occasion of a wrestling bout wherein a Tynedale man and a Coquetwater representative met together, the latter's comrade cry, " Aa'l back wor wattor—aa'l back wor wattor,"—sufficient evidence of the ancient rivalry. The dweller in the level law-abiding days of the latter portion of the 19th Century, may be surprised (and possibly pleased, if the old Adam be not dead within him), to hear that " salmon leistering," or " burning the water," does still occasionally take place in Coquetdale. Still on good occasion does the cresset furtively flame by night above the water, and still the luckless salmon quivers on the leister's prongs. Northumbrians, indeed, cling yet to old customs, and even where the deeds of the " old man " have been " put off," the traditions are still kept up, for now as in the days of the Lord Keeper Guildford, are the inhabitants " great antiquaries within their own bounds."

There will still be some found, when the " Northern Lights " flame in the wintry sky, to tell you that these are " Derwentwater's lights," so named because upon the fatal night of his execution in London the aurora glowed with deeper brilliance upon the vales of Tyne. Still, indeed, is the Northumbrian loth to let slip old custom and tradition, and still, with the burr in his throat, is he βαρβαρόφωνος to the stranger within his gate.

OUR VILLAGE.

O UR village ('wor villeedj,' in the Northumbrian ver-
nacular) is not remarkable for natural beauty,
historical incident, or the physical comeliness of the inhabitants. These be gifts to advantage it from a worldly
point of view, no doubt: as serving as lodestones to
tourists and as matter for the rhapsodising maker of guide
books. But, rightly regarded, they are proved but vanities.

Our village is seated hard by the sea. It caps an
uneven mound that rises like a dyke against the ocean. On
the north the hill climbs higher, shutting out the view, but
keeping the cold winds from the broad links that stretch
away to the shore, the edges broken by sandhills covered
with shocks of coarse, grey-green grass. Beyond is the
sea : here rounding into the curve of the land and there
stretching away to the horizon, where the ships sail
remotely as on a lifted way. That is all. But lack of
natural beauty does not distress us, for we pride ourselves
upon something neither skin-deep nor adventitious: and
that is character. Some years ago a 'clivvor chep' was
down our way, who put things about us into books. This
might have made other folk vain and apt to irritation ; but
we 'sat' for our likenesses, serene in the consciousness
that, like the lady of quality, we should have full justice
done. Besides, as we are always ready with the historic
'skelp i' the lug' (as promised by our countryman to the
Londoner who was uncivil enough to fail to understand his
pronunciation), we have seldom to do without deference :
a certain punctiliousness in its exaction being, indeed, our
sole weakness.

There are three alehouses in the village, and one inn ;
and here it is that the dark foundations are laid for the
eventual building-up of character. Like your excellent
sherris, indeed, that 'good creature ale' hath ever a 'two-

fold operation ' : it is sovran for the green sickness, and
withal it is a most potent influence in the development of
the Ego.   Here is no mistaking one man for another, as in
towns where all men grow alike to a lamentable loss of
interest and a rank sterility of gossip ; for here each
individual hath an idiosyncrasy as naturally as a
patronymic.   The little cluster of houses on either side our
street encloses a world in miniature, with all the types of
the world at large.   Here is the last of an ancient county
family whose fortunes long since decayed.   His house
(which he lets as lodgings in the summer) is still dignified
with pictures of favourite hunters and racehorses ; for his
ancestors spent their substance, in the good Northumbrian
fashion, on cellar and stable.   On Sundays he is majestical
in a tail-coat and a Georgian tie, playing the part of
churchwarden with a courtly grace ; while on week-days
he digs in his garden and ' minds the coo.'   Here is, or
rather here was not long ago, the Common Prodigal : who,
having left his home with his share of his father's goods
(reputed to be a gentleman of family), lived, after the
fashion of prodigals, hobnobbing and drinking 'turn about'
with his inferiors.   Our's was great at arranging sporting
matches and losing his money in them.   He was doubtless
nearing the end of his tether, for he suddenly disappeared,
and is now probably on his way home with that healthy
appetite for the fatted calf which is characteristic of his
breed.   Then for the *bourgeoisie*, here is a merchant from
the neighbour town.   He sustains the appearance of the
country gentleman, is respectfully regarded by the
villagers, whose sporting patron he is, as a ' great pot,' and
has the reputation of being a ' fly man, good at a bargain.'
In the matter of Dissent we vigorously maintain our
strength of character ; for some of us refuse to worship
anywhere. while others—chiefly fishermen and the poorer
sort—are earnest Methodists.   At the little Zion in the
alley there are two local preachers : the one a caretaker
by profession, the other a stonebreaker, both having the
reputation of being ' powerful in prayer ' and excellent at
resisting the devil till he flee from them.   Carnal pride,
intruding here as elsewhere, occasionally lifts a head : as

when the fisherman, in answer to an enquiry (he was seldom visible in church) if he were a 'Methody,' replied, with admirable hauteur, that he was a 'puor-bred Chorchman like his feythors afore him.'

It is natural that, with such a respect for character, we should especially admire all them that are pre-eminent in the matter of idiosyncrasy. Natural that two of us, standing a head and shoulders above the rest, should be held to personify this abstract quality, and so described (admiringly) as 'characters.' The one is commonly, and by his own preference, called 'M—— T——.' He served in Her Majesty's Marines (hence his cognomen), and even now will flourish his cap, with a sound, 'God bless her!' at the very mention of the Widow's name; also, furthermore, if a patron be generous, he will not scruple to be loyally drunk. He represents Bohemianism in its eternal war against respectability, and, as himself remarks, he had leifer sleep 'at the dyke-back than in a dirty lodgin'.' He is thought to be the offspring of a Scottish minister of the straightest sect of the Presbyterians; and, indeed, he does exhibit a great repugnance to being drunk upon the Sabbath. He insists (without regards to the parental reputation) that he was 'born drunk'; but he is a man of sixty, and his memory is scarce to be trusted on the point. He lives partly by odd jobs and partly on a pension: once paid quarterly, but he commuted the half of it, in a moment of peculiar thirst, for a lump sum, money down. Since the new policeman was appointed we have seen less of him than we used. Our other 'character' is—or was, for we are now lamenting his demise—a fisherman, one 'Puffin' Bill,' so named because of his supposed resemblance to the bird. The gossip and the Timothy Tosspot of the village, and furthermore a great authority on sport, his was a striking figure, truly, as he lounged—stooping full six feet —at the corner: with his ragged beard afloat, and his tall felt hat thrust over the thatch of his brows, and his little ring of idlers to whom he would hold forth as one having authority upon every conceivable topic, though with the greatest mastery upon the shooting of wild duck. Laughter

followed where he went, and the shrewder sort would wink
and nudge at his quips. None was keener or quicker to
mark out the V-shaped flight at sea, or to know the spot
where you should lie in wait for it early in the morning or
late, late at e'en. To the very last he would be on the
look-out; and if he saw duck flying high in the air, or
faintly visible under a heavy line of cloud, or low down on
a stormy sea, he would make a point of letting you know
of it. 'D'ye see yon?' he would say, and catch you by
the arm: and the apathy would vanish from his eye, quick
as the upspring of a bird's lid when you startle it from
sleep. 'D'ye see yon?' shading his vision with one hand
and pointing out to sea with the other to a wedged-shaped
flock of birds speeding rapidly northwards against the
wind: 'there's nigh ten brace o' mallards; ay, and mebbe
ye'd get a shot at them the morn out on the rocks a bit
eftor dawn.' Now that he's gone we are by way of dread-
ing lest our reputation for character be held to be on the
wane. Yet we comfort ourselves by reflecting that in this
matter, as with our Northern coal-fields, the substratum
runs so deep that there can be no fear of its being 'worked
out': at all events in our time.

WITH THE NORTH COUNTRY
"METHODIES."

DOUBT may flourish like a green bay, but not in the strong soil of the 'Methodies.' Elsewhere the oracles are dumb, but here they speak with unequivocal directness. Here you shall hearken to a preacher who discourses concerning the 'Maistor' as intimately as a Yorkshireman of 't'owd squire.' The 'Primitives' are the most fervent in praise and the most 'powerful in prayer'; for, being poorer as a rule, and coming closer to the true condition of the Apostles, they are less let and hindered by the carnal impediments that may prevail elsewhere: as, for instance, a choice of words that shall not offend the richer and weaker-kneed. Copper may be the staple of collection, and paraffine the only visible mode of illumination; the breath of the worshippers may hang frosty on the draughts of Little Bethel, yet it will but serve to kindle brighter the flame within. None will be found squeamish where all are poor, and you may call a spade a spade and hurt nobody. Thus, a pitman, when he 'gets religion,' usually becomes a private in the ranks of the 'Primitives.' The bonds of the Church are too narrow for him; the repetition of the Litany is vain in his ears and shrives him not; no confession of miserable sinnership may appease his ardour. It follows, then, that himself must preach, for he is 'under a concern,' as an old-time Quaker would say. He has a personal testimony to give forth unto the world, and he turns to it with a like energy to that he displays in fronting the 'coal face' in the pit. And thus it is he takes service with the 'Primitives,' for a wider space and a larger liberty are here afforded him; with an immediate sphere of influence as well in the 'class-meeting' as in the 'prayer-meeting' after service. The ancient spirit of the North is strong in him; like Hotspur in the matter of love-making, he 'looks not greenly, nor gasps out eloquence, nor hath he no cunning in protestation.' He will kill you some six or seven dozen sins at a 'praying' and think it but 'a trifle, a trifle' and will fall to it at the 'classes' after his day in the pit with a 'Fie upon this quiet life!'

Occasionally, perhaps, it may chance that there is a mistake as to vocation: as with him who, tiring of the discipline of the 'classes,' seceded, and curtly replied to the query of the 'leader' that he was 'dyen wiv' releegion and wis gannin' te join the Chorch.' Unrelieved of book-learning, in the earlier stages he sometimes resembles the Ethiopian courtier who understood not what he was reading; as in the story of him who candidly confessed that he did not know what sort of a 'tree' was indicated by the 'passle-tree' (psaltery); as with that other who, expounding the meaning of the 'gross darkness' in which, according to the Prophet, the people sat, satisfied his audience that that darkness of the mine they knew was as nothing, in comparison, for a gross being twelve times twelve, 'gross darkness' was 'one hundred and fotty-fower times darker than the darkness o' the pit.' But when one putteth forth his hand to the plough it is rare for him to turn back; rather he passes on, from praying and relating his experience at the 'class-meeting' to passing an examination and turning local preacher: when, like an Apostle of old, he goes the rounds and 'confirms the Churches.' Often he is a great reader; daily he searches the Scriptures; his speech teems with quotations from the 'Book.' Nor does he halt if he be a 'bit of a scholar,' but will study the Fathers hard. Or, it may be, he takes a fancy to Milton or Baxter, shining lights of the Puritans, and these shall leaven his discourse with strong yet pleasant old-world savours. His real strength as preacher lies in his intimate knowledge of the daily life and habits of them that 'sit under him.' A fisherman discoursing to fishermen departs but little from his work-a-day occupation: six days in the week he fishes, and on the seventh he casts his nets for men, savouring his utterance with metaphors sweet in the belly of them whose business lies in the great waters.

And so religion becomes a homely and a comfortable thing; being no longer kept for the Sabbath (like best clothes), but rounded to the actual life of day-by-day. A pitman will entrance his hearers by an apt allusion to the pit, and if the pit be what is known as 'fiery,' why, 'twill be odds if he cannot terrify the 'reprobate' by some rich, juicy, and satisfying description of the terrors in store for them.

But it is a mistake to suppose that his staple of doctrine is always terrifying, or that with him, as with Andrew Fairservice, the teaching of other persuasions is held to be no better than 'clauts o' cauld parritch.' Indeed, a certain pitman we know who boldly maintains the very opposite : alleging that inasmuch as he had no benefit of education the 'puir barefoot laddie,' selling matches at the street corner, is in no more parlous case than the preacher himself, who has all the advantages of 'book-larnin'.' Yet the pulpiteers, being strong men, as their hearers are also, do undoubtedly preach not milk for babes but hot meat for the strong. But the very differences amongst them have their comfortable side, and the more nervous in the audience are better sustained by the quiet earnestness of Pratt the shoemaker than by the fiery eloquence of 'Geordie' the pitman : who, after the fashion of a great Scots preacher, seems like to 'ding the pulpit into blads and so flee oot,' whenever he falls to it on the terrors of the Wrath to come.

Sanguine persons rejoice in looking forward to the time when 'meeting-house and kirk, Little Bethel and the Church, Synagogue and Oratory shall be joined together in one large "annexe," and the "Old Man" of Dissent having been "put off," all mankind shall worship harmoniously in the universal church.' But those who know the said 'Old Man of Dissent' know better.

UPON THE ADVANTAGE OF BEING A
NORTH COUNTRYMAN.

DANS le Midi, l'homme du Nord se reconnait à son attitude tranquille, à la concision de son lent parler, tout aussi sûrement que le méridinal se trahit dans le nord pas son exuberance de pantomime et de débit." So writes the historian of the Pays du Midi anent the difference in the respective bearing of Tartarin, the man of the South, and the man of the North, the Duc de Mons.

"C'est la race qui vent ça, jeune homme," says the great Tartarin, "nous sommes tous les mêmes à Tarascon. Du matin au soir, on rit, on chante, et le rest du temps on danse la farandole." There the sun shines ever, and the wind blows softly, rendering life joyous for the Tarasconnais, yet fostering, too, the dreamy imaginative habit, the dislike of realities, that dread disease—'la mensonge.'

But in the colder North another strain is to be met ; there you will find a race, hardy, practical, and unpoetic, lovers of 'les rentes,' keen-nosed as 'bon homme Grandit' for a bargain, conscious as a Scot of the value of "siller," and, above all, inimical to 'la mensonge,' the bane of the Pays du Midi.

So, too, even in Britain, the home of the unemotional, will the North countryman bewray himself by a conciser speech, and greater reserve of manner, while the Southron, with his large loquacity and easy habit, will prove his origin in the colder North.

"Yes," continued Joseph Poorgrass, his shyness, which was so painful as a defect, filling him with a mild complacency now that it was regarded as an interesting study. "'Twere blush, blush, blush with me every minute of the time when she was speaking to me." "Blushes hev been in the family for generations. There, 'tis a happy providence that I be no worse, and I feel the blessing."

"True," said Jacob Smallboy, deepening his thoughts to a profounder view of the subject, "'Tis a thought to

look at that ye might have been worse ; but even as you
be, 'tis a very bad affliction for ye, Joseph."

So speaks the man of Wessex, and between him and the
man from Glasgow what a difference ! " Gude save us,"
said Andrew, " in what can I hae offended your honour ?
Certain a' flesh is but as the flowers o' the field ; but if a
bed of chamomile has value in medicine, of a surety the use
of Andrew Fairservice to your honour is nothing less
evident—it's as muckle as your life's worth to part with
me."

Set these two worthies face to face in the arena, and let
the thumb of the populace decide, and t'will be but short
shrift for the man of Wessex.

'Twas a Scot, of course, who prayed for a ' guid conceit
of hissel'' (and Solomon himself had scarce done better),
while 'twas a Southron that poorly asked to be delivered
from " witches and wizzards, and long-tailed buzzards."
Theologians may quarrel as to the respective degree of
piety involved, yet no one can doubt as to which of the
twain will win the greater carnal success. Your Southron,
indeed, is more loosely joined together ; nature hath forgot
to dovetail his parts with accuracy. Inconsequent he is,
and sidelong as the stealthy crab will he approach the
object of desire. When started upon a descriptive effort
he will choose you the method of the 'circular tour,' and
visit, like the cit abroad, the greatest number of places
possible before ever he attains his goal.

So Andrew Hedger, the Hampshire man, when he
undertakes to show the stranger the way to Diana's house,
wanders here and there in effectual maze for three quarters
of an hour, and finally stops short in rapture, forgetful of
his mission, to gaze upon the pale body of a slaughtered
porker, and—" Ah could eat hog a solid hower ! " says he.

The further North one goes the colder becomes the
climate and the more practical the people. A Yorkshireman will know more concerning a horse (and there is
money in horses) than most mothers about their children ;
the Northumbrian miner knows so well what is not good
for him that he will have nothing to do with a legal eight
hours' bill, notwithstanding the blandishments of the

Socialist, while a Scot with his hereditary wisdom will make a "bawbee" go further than a South countryman a sixpence. The Northumbrian, indeed, may be said to be the younger, or prodigal brother to the Scot, for he loves to early finger his share of his father's goods, and quickly reap a youth's enjoyment, whereas his elder brother over the Border, knowing full well that 'tis as difficult to replace 'siller,' once lost, as to repair a broken skin, is righteously indignant at slaughter of fatted calves. Yet the younger is not to seek, neither, in the matter of worldly wisdom, for he knows right well that there is yet remaining the un-touched moiety of parental goods at home, and thither, when pocket is empty, he quickly hastens.

Apart, indeed, from this quandom recklessness of his (which should be pardoned him, for 'he has it from his father '), the Northumbrian hath many a Scottish quality. His speech is epigrammatic and incisive, his point of view is practical and direct, and what he sets his heart on, that will he acquire.

'Tis with wit rather than humour he practises, and he can deal you a home thrust as shrewdly as the 'pawkiest' Scot, as witness the occasion when the North Tynedale celebrity put the 'meenister,' who had been somewhat foolishly upbraiding him, to an entire confusion thus: "They maun ha' been unco scant o' timmer when they made ye a pillar o' the kirk."

The Southron, on the other hand, with slower mind and humbler nature, hath the greater turn of humour, and here again he is at a disadvantage, for wit is forged for attack, while humour is mainly useful in life's battle for defence.

Down South, again, the forelock may be tugged as the 'Squire' passes, but in the North a nod suffices. Warmth of heart may incline to the side of the Northerner, but the Southerner has the best of the manner.

In the 'North-countrie,' indeed, the small clothes of feudalism have long since been discarded, the last 'clout' having been 'cast' at time of the discovery (dating from 1832) that one man is as good as another. Here the various qualities of a man are scrutinized in a practical business light, are summed up as though 'twere matter for a balance sheet, with auditor's certificate duly attached. Thus 'canny' may with equal ease describe 'my lord' or pot-boy, provided (according to the glossary) either possess 'certain kind, agreeable and useful qualities.' 'Gobby,' again, will pick off a man neatly, though 'twere a difficult word to translate into less than a sentence.

When the celebrated James Pigg, a native, as he proudly proclaimed himself, of 'Paradise, aside Canny Newcassel,' called upon Mr. Jorrocks in answer to his advertisement for a huntsman, he thus characterized his countrymen, " Aye, civil, aye, they're all civil enough gin you're civil to them.   If ye set up your gob, they'll mump it, I's warn't."

Suggestive peculiarities, again, are commonly picked out as relentlessly as amongst schoolboys, for exposure, epithets being terse, and polysyllabics eschewed. 'Tis doubtless a wholesome practice, for it tends to the correction of all undue egotism, and in the case of the sensitive, is of value in cauterizing the part affected.   Up here, indeed, a man wears not his heart upon his sleeve for any daw to peck at, and it may well be that a Northern cuff will indicate as much affection as a Southern kiss.

North-country eulogy seems at first sight, often enough, to be mainly depreciatory, consisting chiefly of negatives, and it is only by applying the Baconian method that one can arrive at the real essence.   Thus, over the Border, if an individual is 'no this, no that,' and 'no t'ither,' it follows 'per exclusionem et rejectionem' that an affirmative basis of excellence will be found for him to stand on at last.

And now, summing up, one may say that the Northerner will usually have the advantage in life's handicap over the Southerner, for his view is narrower, and his horizon is limited by the practical, whereas his fellow-man in the South is as frequently a dreamer.

'Tis doubtless all a question of climate.   In regions where the sun shines warmly the physical needs are less oppressive, and the necessity for exertion smaller, but where the east wind is the vogue, man must exert himself or die of inanition, with the result that the physical activity thus begotten insensibly effects the mental faculties in a like direction.

ON THE FURTHER ADVANTAGE OF BEING
A SCOT.

O N no subject, indeed, have more individuals, even of
acknowledged ability, made a greater number of
mistakes than in treating of the national character of the
Scots people. One would think, indeed, to listen to these
gentry, that some serious disadvantage clung to each
member of that race, that the mere fact of their nationality,
like ignorance of Court in the case of Touchstone's shepherd, sufficed to put them in the same " parlous state."
Again, not only do they show ill-breeding by sneers
directed at the poverty of the race, but they prove their
own mental range to be extraordinarily narrow by assert-
ing, as they vehemently do, that the Scot has no notion of
humour, and but little idea of wit.

One who has been called the " wisest and wittiest of
Englishmen," Dr. Samuel Johnson, was never tired of
levelling his wit, like some clumsy petronel, against the
devoted body of the Scots nation, and yet, (alas for the
inconsistency of human nature !) his chiefest companion
through life was one who came from that detested country.
Another famous English wit was wont to groan in Athenian
fashion over the Bæotia of Scotland, and was even carried
to such lengths by prejudice as to assert that it required a
" surgical operation " to get a joke into the head of a Scot.

The fact is, that the great doctor's prejudice was
due to what he might have himself acknowledged to
be (had it been roundly put to him by a lady) " pure
ignorance, ma'am," while the prejudice of the well-known
clergyman who uttered the above-quoted *mot* was chiefly
due to pique. Because a Scot does not guffaw over
a *mot* is there to be no inward chuckle ? Does one sayer
of " good things " ever care a button or waste a smile over
the *jeux d'esprit* of another ? Of course not. The stranger

in Edinburgh departed disgusted because, amongst a people notorious for pungent wit, incisive epigram, and crushing repartee his own poor humour went unregarded.

I will here at once acknowledge that for humour in the ordinary acceptation of the term the Scot does not greatly care. For the clown and the red hot poker he has something of a contempt. It is skimble shamble stuff, whereas "wut" is a matter of practical significance; the playground of the full-grown man, the delight of the greybeard who has plumbed life's depths, and acquired a correct notion of the value of "siller." Humour, indeed, is poor stuff compared to wit, going frequently, as the learned Mr. Burton discovered, with melancholy, and accompanying a poor opinion of one's self, whereas wit is the *vin brut* of the mind, trodden out of the unadulterated intellect, oozing forth from the winepress of those who have "a gude conceit o' theirselves." If you want a matter put with terseness and conciseness, and neat so as to fit into a nutshell; full of sap, and ripe with knowledge of the depravity of one's neighbour, you must turn to a Scot with his "pawky" wit and biting intellect. Say the notorious failings of womankind are in question, and how tame is the "varium et mutabile semper" of Virgil, how tiresome the long tirades of Juvenal, as compared with the epigrammatic scorn of an Andrew Fairservice. "Na, na; we'll hae nae slices o' the spare rib here, be praised for't," quoth the gardener at Osbaldistone Hall; "the first of his trade having had," as he shrewdly puts it, "eneuch o' thae cattle." Or say, again, that the frequent failure of the preacher to administer comfort from the pulpit is the topic, and where will you find the soul of wit so distinguishable as in the gardener's description of the discourse at the parish church. Four little words suffice to reveal a world of discontent; and "Clauts o' cauld parritch, clauts o' cauld parritch," replied Andrew, with a most supercilious sneer.

"We do not laugh," says a recent writer, "at real humour. It falls upon us with the deliberation of the morning dew. We know not how it comes, but only that it is there." So it is with the humour of an Andrew Fair-

service or an Edie Ochiltree, who to a deliberation like
that of the morning dew join the crushing force of the
bludgeon. After an encounter with such an adversary the
victim may be observed, like Monkbarns after the argument with Edie concerning the Prætorium, to hobble off
discomfited to some retired spot where he can proceed to
bind up his wounded self-respect as best he may.

Yet so inveterate is the prejudice of the Southron that
he will not even allow a Scot the merit of his own accomplishments. Believing in his narrow and foolish fashion
that the Scot, because he does not draw attention with
nudge and wink to his own witty sayings, is therefore
ignorant of their being, he loudly proclaims that he has no
notion of humour ; and, setting up as an authority on the
matter, constitutes himself showman to the wares of
another.

The reason why the Scot permits this intrusion is not
due, of course, to modesty, but to the strong reserve and
self-sufficiency so characteristic of the race. His wit and
humour are no house-top utterances, nor do they require
the stimulus of wine, but quietly they steal forth in the
way of soliloquy and every-day conversation, accompanied
by no advertising laughter, but by an inward chuckling.
He cares not whether the world outside perceives his drift ;
whether it disregards his jokes or makes them its own. It
is enough for him that his table is laid and his own digestion
keen ; whether others join him or no is a matter of indiffer-
ence. Thus, in justice, he should be praised equally for
the philosophy as for the good taste of his attitude, yet the
reward he reaps from the world is an accusation of dulness
of mental faculty. One might, indeed, as well accuse the
lady of quality who without ostentation wears upon her
person costly jewels, of ignorance of their value, as vilify
the Scot because he draws not attention to his adorning
wit.

And now, to turn to the general question whether the
Scot is really disadvantaged, as many believe, by his
hereditary characteristics. The truth is that, if only
prejudice be discarded, it will at once appear that the
supposition is ridiculous and untenable. Granted that he

starts from scratch, owing to circumstances over which he
has no **control, in** the **handicap** of life, his idiosyncrasy is
such **that he eventually** attains the pride of place. The
vulgar **belief, of course, insists that** he is rough-mannered
and **taciturn, lacking versatility,** redolent of the sanctimonious. **Here again, if one regards the matter** rightly, it
will be seen at once that these accusations result from
prejudice, **jealousy and superficial observation.** Virtue,
indeed, is **never popular—never nearly so enchanting to**
the vulgar **as a little wildness. A " douce, responsible**
man," such **as Aristides is hissed off the stage, whilst a**
" pleasure-loving, rake-helly **chiel," such as Alcibiades is**
recalled **by** the groundlings **again and again. If on occasion**
he **be a trifle brusque it** is **because he is so devout a lover**
of **the truth ; if ever a** little **taciturn it is because he is a**
philosopher ; **if** apparently lacking **in** charity it is **that he**
knows **the** majority are " reprobate," unworthy of pearls ;
if ever sanctimonious to **the** outward view, because he loves
piety and the ordinary do not ; while as for versatility, **he**
is, in argument especially, the nimblest of mankind. **" I**
wunner at ye, Bailie," responded the quick official who
was " **heckled** " concerning the **water-supply (early** closing
being the rule of the " toon ") " I wunner at ye talkin' o'
water when it's ten meenits **till ten o'clock."** The Bailie,
needless to say, hastily **adjourned the meeting,** and the
subject of the water-supply **at once became a matter of**
secondary **importance.**

That famous **Scot, the Admirable Crichton, attained, as**
every one knows, **so wide a reputation throughout the**
world of the sixteenth **century for his versatility and variety**
of accomplishments **that his name** has come **down to us as**
a pattern for **all the** ages. **" All** the choicest **and** most
profound philosophers, mathematicians, naturalists, medi-
cinists," &c., we are told, " together with the professors of
arts and disciplines at Paris, studied **and** set their brains
awork how to devise the **most difficult** questions, thereby
to puzzle him in **the resolving of them,** meander him in his
answers, put him **out** of his **medium, and** drive him to a
non-plus." And **yet, so quick and apt was the** Scot, so
endowed with the resources of **his race, that he** kept all
this mighty host **at** bay without **an effort.**

Again, how ridiculous is the belief that a Scot is naturally boorish and ill-mannered. When one reflects upon his characteristics it is apparent at once that the self-confidence with which he is reproached, so far from being a stumbling-block to good breeding, is in reality the crown of good manners. It is only your shy and awkward, diffident and self conscious individual who will never learn what to do or say upon an emergency. The Scot never hesitates by doubting his own capacities, nor commits that grievous sin against good breeding, an apology, but knows what is due to him, and, without any bourgeois diffidence, takes it.

Where would you find better breeding than in the quiet self-possession of an old Aberdeenshire man, gillie and weaver, upon whom one afternoon her Majesty unexpectedly made a call? Informed of the honour done him, out goes John to the carriage-side, in no wise abashed by the scarlet liveries or the presence of Royalty itself. "An' sae ye hae come," was his greeting as he tugged at his forelock, proud as a man might be, but as self-possessed as though he were but welcoming an old friend to tea. Her Majesty descended and visited the small biggin, John acknowledging next day that his wife Mary was "some shy," but he "kenned weel eneuch hoo to talk to that class o' person."

CHILDREN OF BOREAS.

THE suckling of Romulus and Remus by the wolf is not merely an interesting phenomenon in natural history, or a pardonable act of self-advertisement on the part of that far-seeing animal, but an important fact to the scientist of to-day who explains so much by means of "hereditary tendencies." He will see, of course, in the ferocity of the Roman soldier evidence of ancestral influence, and, similarly, we perhaps may trace the special type of character to be met with in Northumberland to the rough nursing of Boreas. The southerner who sojourns there is often somewhat puzzled and offended by an apparent lack of social courtesy—of the "s'il vous plait" of life. He will dislike to have his own "good evening" responded to by a gruff nod from "Geordie the pitman" on his homeward way, and it is not till he comes to closer touch that he can recognise the warmth of the heart under Geordie's jacket.

Three main traits of character and one shibboleth seem ingrafted in the Northumbrian nature: a mighty determination and a certain resulting ruggedness, a keen love of sport, a great capacity for liquor, and a curious phonetic difficulty with the letter "r." These are the four leading "habits"—to use a gardener's phrase—of the Northumbrian character, found alike amid the older gentry, the industrial population, the pitmen, the Tynedale lads, and the fishermen along the coast. They seem, indeed, to have given up all hope of ever conquering the letter "r." They begin by rolling it, like the Scots, then in despair are fain to swallow it; the result being the well-known "burr" by which the Northumbrian is bewrayed. Their determination, however, (apart from the matter of this little "r") is clearly shown in every other walk of life, and is especially manifested in politics and sport.

The working classes, of course, are almost to a man Gladstonian Radicals ; and having once made up their minds on any point (which is done pretty quickly) nothing will induce them to listen to the other side of the question. One trial is enough to convince even the most persistent and stout-hearted that their conversion is impossible. As to the love of sport of all kinds the daily challenges in the local newspapers are evidence of how deep a root it has in the northern heart. Here you read that " I, A.B. will match my pigeon to fly any pigeon in Newcastle, 1 mile to 3 miles, for £10 a side,"—and next, " I, B.C., am astonished at D. of Pity-me, wanting to shoot me after the last match. I will shoot him at 30 pigeons each ; gun below elbow, elbow down, &c., &c." There is no difficulty for the willing sportsman ; he has but to pre-pay his challenge and name his fancy—rabbit coursing, sparrow-shooting, boxing, whatever he may choose, and a competitor will instantly confront him. It is "sport" rather than athletics to which the Northumbrian is devoted, and he dearly loves (after the time-honoured fashion of sportsmen everywhere) to back his opinion with money. " Geordie, the pitman " is, perhaps, typical in this respect, being always ready with his " brass " to back his fancy. " At Pitch and Toss," one writer says, " I have seen a pitman who won £70 in one afternoon lose the whole of it next day in betting on the bowling on Newcastle Town Moor, and go to work the next day afterward guiltless of the ownership of sixpence."

He may usually be known by his dog, for without one he feels, according to the well-known story, "sae stark neaked like." It is often a greyhound for coursing hares, or if that be too expensive, a mongrel for rabbits. Then again, he is a pigeon fancier, and ofttimes you may meet him carrying in his hand a square wooden box with perforated top, containing his homing pigeon, or perhaps he has his bird fast in his hand to fly it from a nearer flighting place. An ardent pigeon-flyer had the question of the Church's disestablishment presented to him in a very attractive light, when it became evident to him that he might possibly attain possession of the porch's architrave to strengthen therewith his beloved "pigeon-ducket" (pigeon-cote). And it is well known that another, when lying on his deathbed and listening to a discourse concerning the metamorphoses that await the true believer in another world, startled the clergyman by asking him if he would have wings too. "Ye-es," replied the clergyman, somewhat taken aback; with all humility, he trusted he might say so. "Then," said Geordie, eagerly, the old Adam flashing forth, "a'll flee thee for a sovereign." If, again, Geordie happens to be of a quieter turn of mind, he becomes a great gardener, proof of which is that a certain variety of pink claims him as "eponymos." Sometimes he is a poultry-fancier; and if he takes to music he will make noise enough for an entire orchestra. This same energy is also proven when he is in for a drinking bout on "pay-Saturday," as it is called. This is his opportunity when his fortnightly wages are jingling "cannily" in his pocket. Then, indeed, does he show his descent from the valiant ale-quaffers and mead-champions of a more northerly North.

Yet, though a deep drinker, he is no tippler. He is not in the habit of fuddling himself, as unfortunately some of his neighbours are. His work is too hard to admit of that, and his mind is too broad and his energies too vigorous to submit to such frittered and slovenly ways. "Canny Newcassel" itself, as a town, ranks very high in the class lists of drunkenness. "Proxime accessit" may describe with fair accuracy her position, while throughout the country the ancient devotion to strong drink prevails. Race-week, the last week in June, is of course the great event of the year. It is then that the Carnival of the North is held, and work there is next to none. Pits are laid idle, and factories are stopped or work "short-time." Banks close at 1 p.m. each day, and not long after, partner and clerk may be seen cheek by jowl in the enclosures, enquiring "the odds." Any good horse owned by a local man is generally made favourite by the populace. But he must really be a good one, for the knowledge of horseflesh is well diffused.

Such are the more obvious characteristics of Northumbria, and as they are now so have they been for centuries.

We may note the same eager and determined spirit in the defiance that brought upon the land the terrible punishment of William the Conqueror, traces of which are to be seen to this day. In the same way we may explain the marauding, raiding, reiving that went on continuously till the accession of James VI. of Scotland; and the cock-fighting, bull and bear baiting, and heavy potations of a later day all testify to the same strong strain of blood and tradition.

TALES.

GEORDIE NICHOLSON.

THE stranger who, perchance, may have wended his way some Saturday afternoon along the broad road leading due north from the town of Oldcastle, will, doubtless, have been surprised at the evolutions of a squad of black figures, thickly packed upon the centre of the bleak common, wide-spreading on his left. Now they are massed together, thick as a swarm of flies; anon they unbind and straggle off in knots of two or three, only, however, to re-form, after an interval, thickly as before. Occasionally, a half-clad active figure may gleam amidst the throng, then suddenly there is motion and commotion, and a hoarse shout breaks upon the air. If the wayfarer be curious, and approach nearer, the sounds of mighty oaths will din upon his ears, another step or two and he will find himself amid a throng of North-country pitmen, hot upon the primeval game of " bowls." Heroes of old time may well have sported at such a game as this, fit pastime for men of brawn—for the " bool " is of heavy stone, needing a strong arm to cast rightly, lovingly rounded, cupped for the fingers' grip—so the stranger may well believe, as he watches the pitman rushing side-long to the mark, and then with a mighty jerk heave his " bool " along the plain. The heavy ball crashes through the air, claps upon the turf, and speeds away in the direction of the white flag in the distance. For a moment or two silence ; then, as the " bool " creeps up and perchance shoots past the other, the air is rent with confused excited cries, through which, like meteors, flash the mighty oaths, strong utterances of strong men . . . . . . On a certain September afternoon the excitement was intense upon this bleak and windy moor, for Geordie Nicholson and Jimmy Straughan were matched for £50. Jimmy had led all along the track, and now his " bool " lay within fifteen yards of the handicap mark. The "bookies" were offering 3 to 1 against Geordie, as he took up his 20 oz. bowl for his last cast; gravely he consulted with his "marrow" (mate) who "trigged" for him on this eventful day, carefully noted the indicated line, preluded first, then with a mighty rush shot forth the heavy ball of stone. Lightly it lit and bounded onwards, rolling without impediment over the uneven turf; now it had crept up to where the other lay, but tottered for a moment on the rising ground, then, staggering over, rolled onward to lie dead, two feet over the winning line. A shout as of Valhalla rent the air—Geordie had won. Backers and fielders, winners and losers crowded round with one accord, vying in congratulations, for such a cast as this had never been known within the memory of man.

"Eh, maw canny hinny," quoth Geordie's "marrow" in an ecstasy, his eye dim with unaccustomed moisture, "maw canny hinny, damn thee, but thoo's a jool; an' noo lads," he continued without pause, wiping away the moisture from his eye with his sleeve, and turning to the throng around him, "had awa' te the public an' wor Geordie 'll gie ye a'al a boose." So the company trooped off in the natural direction, discussing the mighty deed, while Geordie, having donned his upper garments, followed after, his "marrow" clinging to him as half afraid his hero, after such a feat, might be wafted away from him Valhallawards. A fifty pound note was duly handed to the hero by the obsequious landlord, and as it was "pay Saturday," and in addition to his well won bets, his fortnightly wages were jingling in his pocket, Geordie was a rich man that afternoon.

It might thus have been supposed that he would have made a "night of it," but he seemed curiously pre-occupied, and it was soon evident that he was otherwise disposed, for having sat and drank awhile, he whispered his "marrow" to order a "machine" preparatory to going home.

The assembled company looked at each other knowingly as Geordie gave his commands, nudging one another with the elbow as though the secret of Geordie's departure was well-known to them all, though maybe a delicate matter within the length of Geordie's arm. Indeed, amid the general admiration for the hero there seemed to mingle commiseration, as for some weak spot in his character.

The "machine" arrived, he paid the reckoning, (a goodly item) and slipped away with his sorrowful "marrow," who inwardly groaned over such waste of opportunity.

The cab rattled away homewards, and Geordie sank back into his corner nursing a secret joy. 'Twas not that he was so much elated at his triumph, as overjoyed at what the triumph had brought with it. For now he could pour into his Dinette's lap full seventy pounds of "brass," for 'twas of Dinette he had been thinking the afternoon through, and 'twas her, not his "marrow," he had seemed to see before him as he gripped his "bool" for his last victorious throw. Had it not been for that, never had he vanquished "Jimmy," the champion of Bromilaw Colliery— and then, as ever in his happiest moments, his thoughts turned back to the glorious day when he had taken her for his wife, exactly a month agone. How she had ever married him he had never quite understood, but blindly accepted his happiness, and fearfully joyed over it, daily in the depths of the pit as he hewed, and nightly when he woke and found her sleeping beside him. He minded how she had said one evening she was tired-like of the theatre life, and had looked at him a wee-bit sideways, and at once a mighty flame swept upward through him, driving his heart to his lips with a leap, and he had won, ay, won, just as he'd won the bowling match, not knowing how—a flash, a mist over the eyes, a year-long moment, and there was the "bool" across the mark. How well he minded, too, the first time ever he saw her in the theatre, as she danced in the glare of the foot lights; how with lusty lung he had helped to recall her again and again, and how—the wondrous luck of it all—he had chanced to meet her at the house of a far-away cousin of his who lived in the "canny toon." Ay, and then to find to his wonderment that he was even a kind of relation of hers—he, a "proper caution," a great "gowk" of a pitman, she, neat as a fairy, trim as a bird i' the spring, the joy of the theatre, treading a-tip-toe like a star at night.

Her mother, whom he remembered to have "heard tell of," was a "clivvor lass;" had risen to be a teacher, and married a "frenchy chep" who taught the violin, and thus it was that his Dinette spoke a little foreign like, and was so different from every other lass in the world. Ay, that she was, he thought delightedly, as different as cheese from chalk; and then how strong she was too, though to look at her ye'd think she'd snap in two in the hand like a blind worm as ye pick it up. He laughed aloud as he called to mind how she had once caught up in her little hands "ill-tongued Janet" (who'd come in and set up her "impittance"), carried her to the doorway and dropped her into the road, her screeching all the time like an "aad hen gannin' te hev its neck wringed." Again he laughed aloud, for his "marrow" had fallen asleep, and they were nearing home. Then the cab stopped and out the two got, and Geordie gave "good neet" to his sorrowful "marrow," who, knowing his hero would be visible no more that evening, inwardly cursed the "furrin' lass" who kept such a grip on his Geordie.

Geordie had hoped to find his Dinette in, but when he reached his house, the topmost of the long row, it was empty. No matter, she'd likely not yet got back from the town where she had gone to market, and in the meantime he would go out himself to the dene, four hundred yards or so away, and see if there were any rabbits in the gins he had set the night before. Wending his way along, his happiness so overpowered him that he fell to thinking again by way of relief why 'twas she'd married him; 'twas just his strength she'd a fancy for, it could be nowt else, there was nowt in him but that; ay, for did she not use to pinch his arm and say, "Geordie thinks 'tis his, ah, the poor Geordie, but 'tis mine, and 'tis I can hew in the pit, and play the box better than them all."

Wrapped in his delights he carelessly went forward through the wood, till suddenly he stumbled over something that caught his feet in the path, heard a piteous squeak below him, and there in the gin was a struggling rabbit. Why, he was gey an' lucky that afternoon, and stooping down he plucked forth the rabbit, and, breaking its neck with one swift stroke, thrust it into his pocket, prepared to turn homewards. But just as he rose up again, a figure some eighty yards higher up in the wood struck his eye,—why, 'twas she, his Dinette of course. He was about to shout, when at the moment his eye caught sight of another figure leaning carelessly against a tree trunk beside her—that of a man—and as he looked, chill fear caught at his heart. Who was it? Who could it be? She'd ever kept all the men at a distance, and had nowt to say to any of them; not that he mistrusted her for a moment—but—who could it be? He could see the two figures distinctly against the sunset's light, and could catch their frequent laughter as they talked. The man was fat, was adorned with trinkets, and was leering—he noted with a thrill of wrath—right into Dinette's face. A swaggerer, ay, and a "waster;" soft fleshed—a Jew likely, ugh! seemed, too, he'd seen him before somewhere, ah—now he had it, and Geordie dashed his hand across his eyes in an agony, 'twas one of those theatre chaps— manager or such like—come to 'tice her back. A venomous smile crossed Geordie's lips as he thought how easily, if that was the chap's game, he could end it—one twist of the hand on that fat neck of his, and his business would be finished. Stealthily he drew nearer, unperceived through the thick cover, till he could over-hear what was said; he was not one to judge too soon, but to give every man his chance.

As he crouched behind a clump of elder, Dinette's voice came distinctly to him searing his very heart's blood. His lips turned to an ashy green, a rattle sounded in his throat like that of a dying man—'twas she then—his Dinette, sickened with marriage, had sent for the chap to take her away—not he who had tracked her out. What was he to do? Rushing forth from his shelter, should he seize and strangle her there and then? Ay, that would he,—yet no, he could not, and her so beautiful. Rage dropped like a stone through the cold depths of his despair.

"Bravo, bravo," shouted the manager loudly, almost close beside him, as Dinette fell to curtsy and to strut in front of him with wreathed hands and smiling face.

"Bravo, bravo," cries the manager, "encore, encore, every throat from pit to gallery hurraying, and never an empty seat in the house."

Greedily, like a wild beast, Geordie watched her as she passed to and fro, and as he watched, a righteous anger seized hold upon him. Slowly she danced unconscious towards him, swaying delightedly this way and that, kissing her hand as to a lover in the distance, now challenging with eye and lip, then timid and all a-droop like a flower; and now she was within a yard of him. There came a sudden crash through the bushes, a cry of alarm sounded, and Geordie stood face to face with her, so set and impenetrable a look on his grave countenance, that an involuntary terror seized her. Fool that she had been not to have stolen away an hour sooner, was the thought that flitted through her mind as she waited for Geordie to speak. "An' se thoo wes gannin' te flit fre me?" said he slowly, speaking with a thick constrained utterance, "an nivvor se much as te say good-bies, an' ye ma wedded wife?" There was a space of silence, for Dinette did not reply, but stood with downcast eyes toying nervously with her dress.

"An' can ye hev forgotten that this day a month agone we swore te luv an' cherish each the other till death did us part? ay, scarce a month agone, an' yet ye've forgotten, or else ye perjored yorsel that day. Which is it then, for it mun be wan o' the two?" and Geordie's voice had such solemnity, that the manager, who stood by breathlessly listening, grew nervous as to how this strange scene was to end. "No, no, Geordie," Dinette replied, with a sudden rush of words, "I've not forgotten, but ye were so strong, Geordie, and I was ill at the time, and weak, and tired of the theatre life for a space, and 'twas pleasant to think I'd a man to myself that was stronger than them all, and yet I could conquer him with my little finger. Yes, I was weak and tired, Geordie, an' when ye spoke like that, and said I was a queen to ye, an' night and day would ye toil for me, an' a smile would reward ye, ye tempted me, Geordie; if it could only be 'yes,' ye said, then the whole world might go a beggin' for ye, for ye were heart satisfied. Why then I said 'yes,' not thinking, for your eyes were beseeching me like a wild thing's, as tho' for life, an' I couldn't say 'no.'"

"Ay," replied Geordie slowly, and this time there was something uneven in his voice, "Ay, surelies aw did, an' aw spake heart's truth then, an' swore te the same faithfullies before the priest an' in the sight o' Heaven—whiles ye—ye swore te,—yet 'twas a perjory." And here his voice grew strong again till his words rang like a challenge in his listeners' ears.

Again there was a space of silence, then Dinette commenced to tap her foot impatiently upon the ground. What had she to do with grave and serious matters? Life should go ever gaily as a dancing tune, full of warmth, and merriment, and love. What had she to do with frowns, and oaths, and perjury? So she reflected with increasing irritation. Then quickly she replied : "And did I ever think ye would treat me so? and rate me like a school girl thus? Ah, no, not when ye made me promise to marry ye, but soon I found the time would come when we would be quarrelling, an' this is why I'm leavin' ye, Geordie, to spare ye this. I was for goin' unawares to ye. Aye, Geordie, we've made a mistake, we're not suited, for I cannot stay still in the same place always, but love change, and the theatre, and the applause of many, not of one—yes, that's the truth of it, an' if ye ask why I married ye, 'tis as I said—ye persuaded me, Geordie, an' frightened me into it, once ye had me in those strong arms of yours. Yes," she continued, gaining courage as she went on, "and 'tis certain I'd have gone before, but he," pointing to the manager who was standing stock still in amazement at the scene that was being played before his eyes, "was away down south and could not come for me, and 'twas amusing, too, to see the other men's wives here in the village copying me in the way of walking and talking, and in their manner of dress ; to see them stepping high, and holding up their gowns as they crossed the road"—and here she fell to mimicking an awkward strut, then suddenly stopped short to break into a ripple of laughter—"Yes, 'twas entertainment indeed, and then how they hated me while always they were for imitating me,—that was the most amusing of all."

At every fresh and unconscious revelation of her heartlessness, Geordie's face grew paler and more stern, and now he spoke again.

"An' se forgettin' aal that's passed atween us ye're bent te leave me by maa lane? Na, na, it canna be, Dinette," and here his voice broke away in a sob, and he fell upon his knees before her, " ye canna dee't, lassie, an' me clean daft for ye ; wey, lassie, aw won the great match on the toon moor this eftornoon, an aal wi' thinkin' o' your bonny fyece, that might tempt an angel to gie up heaven for ye ; see, lass, the brass aa've won for ye," and he pulled out a handful of sovereigns, and poured them on the grass at her feet. "Na, na, ye'll cyum back hyem wi' me, an' think what a feast we'll hev the neet ; a singin' hinny, an' aal that's canny, cyum awa, ma hinny," and he spread out his arms imploringly.

With an increased impatience she drew herself away from him, for she was fearful again now, his passion frightening her, and she so eager to depart. " No, no, Geordie, 'tis good-bye," she replied hastily, "an soon ye'll be forgettin' me, an' thinkin' 'twas all a dream of the night."

" Na, lass, a'll no," said Geordie slowly, as he rose to his feet, his face whiter than before, but so fixed and resolute that instinctively she shrank before him. "Tell me then," he continued, and his voice was calm again, and his whole bearing betokened an absolute self-possession, as of a settled purpose, " if ye will no come back wi' me, will ye let me cyum wi' ye, an' tend ye, an follow ye about tiv all the theatres and plyces ye gan' te ? "

" No, no, ye cannot, I tell ye," replied she, with a spasm of anger, his resoluteness terrifying her, " I cannot play, and dance, and sing when all the time I'm tied to ye, an' stifled with bondage ; can a bird sing i' the cage ? no, no, no, I tell ye, ye cannot," and her voice rose shrilly upwards in despair, for Geordie's face moved not nor showed any sign of understanding. " An' if ye ask again why I married ye," she went on heartlessly, for Geordie made no answer, " why I've told ye, an' if that will not satisfy ye, then I know not—'twas but a momentary folly—I cannot tell—je suis artiste—oui, oui,—nay more, I am a woman," she murmured proudly to herself, as she glanced down her beautiful form to her delicate feet. "And am aw no a man ?" came from Geordie's lip in turn, "ay, am aw, as ye could hev seen on Newcassel Moor this eftornoon, ay, aw am that," he repeated, with a proud simplicity, "and no te be thrown awa' like an aad shoe when maybies ye've walked thro' the mud wiv' it. 'Twes not for that I swore te ye te luv' and cherish ye in sickness an' in health till death did us part, a month since, an' 'twes in real ornest before the altar that aw myed the oath ; ay, an' a'll keep to it. Ay," he repeated solemnly, as he strode towards Dinette, who sank in terror to the ground, and each word sounded slow and solemn as a knell, " A'll keep to it, for 'twas till death did us part." Gently he picked her up from the ground, and folding her to his bosom, walked rapidly away uphill through the wood. And now the manager, starting from his trance, followed after and endeavoured to stop his progress. " Put her down, man, put her down, she's coming away with me, man, I'm sorry for ye, but she's signed an engagement." Geordie's strong right arm came sweeping round in reply, and hurled the speaker from his balance backward over into the brush-wood. There he lay quaking till the memory of the look on Geordie's face aroused him to action. Plucking himself from out of the bushes, he stood up and commenced to holloa so loudly for help, that immediately a number of pitmen and their wives came thronging from the village to discover the cause of the outcry. Hurriedly the frightened manager related what had happened, and pointed out the direction in which Geordie had gone. Geordie's " marrow" was amongst the number of the new comers, and, dimly realising the gravity of the situation, at once set off in the direction indicated. " Wor Geordie's a tarr'ble chep when he's vext, aw doresent think what may hev happened," he murmured to himself, as he strode onward through the wood. Soon he came upon an open space, in the centre of which lay a quarry hole, long since disused, wherein an unknown depth of water had gradually accumulated. And there, on the very brink, lay a cap, which the searcher, with a thrill of fear, recognised to be Geordie's. Overcome by a feeling of terror, he staggered to the broken edge, and looked over on to the dark waters below. The sullen surface broken into small uneven waves strengthened his suspicions, and there, right in the centre of the pool, as if to render further doubt impossible, floated the bright bonnet of a woman.

THE HERD OF WINDYHAUGH.

IT was with some reluctance that I finally accepted, towards the latter end of November, some fifteen years ago, my uncle, the Border herd's, invitation to bring my books and stay with him a few days. He had always been regarded as somewhat "uncanny," and latterly his idiosyncrasies were reported to have developed. But as my uncle had no children and was known moreover to have saved money (he was said to be cleverer with sheep than any other two shepherds together in Coquetdale), worldly wisdom and my father's pressure determined my going. I was still attending sessions at Edinbro' University with a view to the ministry, and as my exit examination was fast approaching, and my father had but little gear of his own, it was to my uncle (after whom I had been named) that he looked to give me a start in the world. It was thought, too, that eventually I might, through his influence and that of his relations, who formed a numerous clan in the dale, receive a "call" to the kirk at Shawbottle, of which they one and all were members.

There was nothing really formidable about my respected uncle, and his cottage was a magnificent place for uninterrupted study, lying as it did some nineteen miles from the central village where the marts were held, and situated amongst the lonely dales where sheep and their attendant shepherds were the only dwellers. Still, I had always an uncomfortable feeling when staying with him, though I saw little of him save in the evenings. Rarely, indeed, did I feel at my ease with him, for he never left practising on my feelings, and was always endeavouring to discover a joint in my harness wherein his crafty wit might enter. He loved to probe into my heart, to discover what I thought of him, and whenever he made a mention of the money he had saved, screwing up his eyes he would watch me out of a sly corner. Add to this that he was often extremely absent in his manner and was wont to mutter to himself at times in very disconcerting fashion, and 'twill be acknowledged that he was not the pleasantest companion in the world for a sensitive youth with but little capacity for concealing his emotions.

Then again, the last time I was with him, his previous cold and sneering treatment of his wife had shown signs of a fast development into an active aversion, and I misliked the notion of again playing audience to an unfair combat. My aunt, indeed, having but little strength of character, and possessed of no great mental equipment, was an open target for his wit, the very booty of his scorn.

She had grievously disappointed him, I believe, by bearing him no issue, and, realizing she was no longer beloved, the spirit had gone out of her, so that she resembled, as a woman will when affection is dead, a faded flower, the scentless presence of which is but a mournful memento of decay.

I fell to wondering as I trudged onwards over the bleak slopes of Monzie Law if she still decked herself out of an evening in the scraps of finery that once perhaps had pleased a lover's eye, but now did but serve to provoke sarcastic comment and disdain.

This vanity of hers was indeed the sole interest she had left in life; once doubtless she had been beautiful, and she still clung to this forlorn memory in spite of her husband's scorn.

I had plenty of opportunity for reflection upon this solitary walk, for it was full nineteen miles from Jedburgh town, where I lived with my father and sisters (my mother had died a few years after my birth), to my uncle's cottage, which sheltered on the slope of Windyhaugh, a spur of the Cheviot range. By three of the afternoon, however, I had broken the back of my task, and was climbing the high slope between Wedder Hill and Monzie Law. Half-an-hour more and I was amidst the reaches of upper Coquetdale, and, occupied with fresh thoughts concerning my uncle, fell to a more leisurely procedure.

Surely, I thought, if a man were inclined to be peculiar,

this would be the very country to enhance his foibles. The rounded hills, that rolled away in vast monotony of grey-green colour, were as destitute of variety as billows of a stormy sea. Save for the lonely sheep, and the solitary curlew, or a rare figure on a hill-top, whose back aslant and length of stride proclaimed him a shepherd, no sign of life was visible.

Often, when he could not get to the "meeting" on the Sabbath, my uncle, as I knew, would go for a fortnight without any intercourse, save for the chance "crack" upon the hillside, with his fellowmen. This loneliness would, I felt, have been unendurable to one who, like myself, was used to cities, and to feel the warmth of human fellowship blow on every side of him, and I felt certain it must have a peculiar force in the developing of character. The tinge of melancholy, which in my uncle's family had grown to insanity, it was said, in the case of his grandfather, might surely have been caused by this isolation of existence. He it was who, smitten with disgust at life, had one summer forenoon thrust his crook deep into the ground, tied thereto his plaid, and twisting the end round his neck, had slowly, and inch by inch, as it were, strangled himself with the coolest deliberation in the world.

There was, again, a good deal of the old reckless Border spirit still surviving amongst the inhabitants of these lonely dales, which would naturally foster the harsher side of a man's character. I had once accompanied my uncle upon a "salmon leistering" foray, one dark October night, and I well remembered the fierce excitement of his mood, as salmon after salmon was speared and flung upon the bank.

Perhaps, it was the quieter blood in my veins derived from my father, who, though he had settled down as a draper in Jedburgh, was South-country born and bred, that rendered me timid, or it may have been the unaccustomed solitude of my surroundings, but certainly it was with no expectation of enjoyment, but with a foreboding as of some impending disaster, that I descended the fell to where, upon the haugh, my uncle's shieling stood.

As I knocked upon the door I heard the growl of a collie within, and knew my uncle must have returned from the hill side; another moment and he opened the door himself to me.

He did not seem much altered, though it was two years since I last had seen him; a thread or two of grey appeared in the thick of the ruddy beard, and the ragged ends of it had somewhat faded.

My aunt, however, had certainly changed; she had grown thinner, and her listless manner had an occasional turn of fear in it. Could my uncle, tiring of his ironical method, have taken to actual ill-treatment of her? I determined to watch and find this out for myself, for my aunt would never confide in me, believing me a favourite with my uncle.

It was early yet when I arrived, and, after having made me drink off a large mug of milk, my uncle took me out again to inspect two cows that had recently been sent him. So successful had he been with his master's sheep, that, in addition to his "pack-wage" as shepherd, he had been presented with these two cows as a testimony to his services. His master's "hirsel" numbered some fifty score, and scarce a ewe or a lamb had he lost the preceding year.

Having duly inspected the cows we turned indoors again, and made our supper of scones and cheese made of ewes milk. My uncle, I noticed, never once spoke to my aunt, who sat apart in the ingle-nook, listlessly gazing into the fire the evening through. It was evident that the breach between them had widened since last I was there, for my uncle now took no notice at all of his wife, no longer even amusing himself with subtle scorn and sarcasm at her expense. The meal over, my uncle sat back in his chair, and lighting his pipe, commenced to question me in his old fashion concerning hogs and gimmers, wedders and ewes, for he loved ever to catch me tripping over the various distinctions of his trade. Inwardly I believe he was proud of having as nephew one who had been trained up as a "scholar," for he himself had had practically no "larnin'," yet such was his curious turn of mind that he delighted to lay bare my ignorance, no matter how or where, and then, with a chuckle, would remark that in his young days a body could grow up as ignorant as may be without wasting "ower muckle siller" on the job.

We went to bed early, for the next day being the Sabbath, we were to walk over the hills to the " meeting " at Shawbottle, some nine miles distant, and it was necessary to start soon after eight o'clock.

The morning came, and with it a sudden change of weather. Over-night it had been clear and bright, but to-day the sky was overcast with heavy clouds, and my uncle foretold a snowstorm before night.

Still he was determined to go, and we started shortly after eight, leaving my aunt behind without ever a word from my uncle.

From his conversation as we climbed the steep slopes of the opposite hills it appeared that my uncle had suddenly taken a religious turn; formerly he had always attended " meeting " for the sake of the " crack " with his friends afterwards, but now he went, it appeared, for the sake of the " preachin' " and his inward comfort.

I could scarce keep from wondering what it was that had caused this change, for I had ever been somewhat sceptical on the phenomena of sudden conversions, having seen many curious and unlooked for results from the same. To my mind religion, being of a more serious nature than anything else in the world, should be a matter of an advised selection and a life-long training, yet here were people who would inform you that their whole nature was changed in an hour's space, the habits of a life-time cast aside, and they on an instant become " new creatures," as though the past of a man were but the finger of a clock, to be shifted this way and that upon a hasty computation. No light was shed upon the subject, however, till after the " meeting " was over, and we had got well on our homeward journey, when my uncle at last broke the long fit of silence that had held him since leaving the kirk. We were sitting on the lee side of a " stell " at the time, eating a frugal luncheon, when he thus commenced :

" I'm thinkin' the meenister did not get a reet haud o'

his subjeck the day, the fall o' man is a graun' subjeck for a discoorse, though reetly it should be ca'ad the fall o' woman, for 'twas she that fell, draggin' the man along wiv her, the jade. St. Paul noo wud ha dyen bettor wiv it, for he wes na marrit, an' he kenned weel enow the monstrous natter of a woman, whiles the meenister, puir body, is far ower muckle marrit to mak' a guid job o' a tex' like that."

" Man," he burst out with sudden ferocity, bringing his fist with a clap down upon his knee, " I pairfeckly loathe the hail race of fyemales ! To think o' losin' Paradise through the folly of a woman,—aal for an' aeple, tee,—'tis a thocht that drives me a'most wild—an aeple," he slowly repeated with intensity of scorn, " an' aeple, whey, t'wud tak' siller to tempt a man,—a mort o' siller might hae' even tempted me, but there wud hae' been some sense i' that, for dootless it wud hae' been permitted to tak' it wiv one off the premises." " Ay," he repeated again in solemn tones, " I pairfeckly loathe the hail race o' fyemales, their only use is to bring bairns into the world, and when they canna dee that, whaurs the use o' them ?" " I'm no muckle o' a scholar, as ye ken," he continued, in quieter tones, " but I made up a bit poetry on the subjeck some time back, wi' the help o' the paraphrases an' a young chep that was up the wattor on a walkin' tower, as he ca'd it, an' lodged wi' me twa neets ; he wes a gey clivvor chep tee, a scholar frae Oxford College, an' kenned aal aboot poetry an' sich like predicaments, an' was a wunnerful help to me ower the job. I kenned weel that twa ends of the paraphrase should match, the y-ane the t'ither, like the lugs of a y'ewe, but hoo to catch a haud o' them was beyont me. Man, it wes a tarr'ble fashions job, an' I'd hae gien it up had it no' been for the scholar. Ye'll no believe it, maybe, but he tell't me poetry wes as common at Oxford as grin'stanes i' canny Newcassel. I did'na tell him though what 'twas for I wanted it," continued my uncle, slyly, " but I howked it oot o' him fine wivoot his ever suspectin' onything at aal. Ay, I did sae, an' here's the poetry," and he commenced forthwith to sing, as though at kirk, the following words :

> "The deidly sarpint lauchin' crept
> To Eden's fair gyardin,
> For weel he kenned a woman is
> Aye ready for to sin.

An' helter-skelter loupit Eve
  Into the trap o' sin.
Whence, for her fyulishness man aye
  Mun sweat an' groan within "

" The hail race o' them," he remarked bitterly, as he
concluded his singing, " are just aal Eve's at bottom ;
" aye ready for to sin," hits em off fine, an' the sly deil he
kenned it weel enow."

" But uncle," I here remarked somewhat incautiously,
" you got married yourself." He turned upon me with a
snarl. " An' mebbe ye're thinkin' ye've got a haud o' me
there, but ye hanna, for there's twa good reasons for't ;
forst, she had siller, an' second, I was no releegious then,
but I am the noo, an sair, sair hae I repentit ma folly !
But I bear up weel, for releegion's a gey guid comfort i'
misfortune. Sorch the Scriptor weel, an' ye'll be sure to
find what ye want. An' what does Scriptor say aboot the
onfaithful woman ? Whey, " gie her a writtin' o' divorcement," it says, an that's what I'm gannin' te dee. D'ye
mind that good-like nowt, Airmstrong, the shepherd that
dwells by Naked Law ? He's been jest constant aboot ma
hoose an' ma wife syne the back end o' the year, but I'll
nae allow it, my man. There's to be nae breakin's o'
commandments i' ma hoose ; the smoke o' hell shall nivvor
smirch ma garments, I tell ye, " Let them rather marry
than burn," says Scriptor, an' sae I'll marry them at aince,
aye, this very neet if sae be as I catch him in by on my
return."

" But uncle," I remonstrated, amazed at his fierceness
of tone, and alarmed by the wildness of his eye, " you can't
marry them, in the first place you'd have to get a divorce,
if that were possible, as I'm sure its not, for my aunt's
never done an ill deed in her life, of that I am quite
certain, and then——"

" Haud yer tongue," burst in my uncle, " I tell ye I
will marry them, I'll gie her a writtin' o' divorcement, an'
we'll aal sign it, an' then I'll marry them tegither, 'tis plain
as dayleet, an' but followin' oot the Scriptor injunctions.
'Tis a peety tho' that ye're no a full fledged meenister yet,
or we cud hae dyen the job better nor ivor. But ye can

mak' up the writin',' for ye're a scholar, sae there may be some use in ye efter aal."

I made no answer to this, for I scarce knew what to believe. Indeed, I feared my uncle was really insane, for I never for a moment believed his calumny concerning his wife, and I could but conjecture that the whole story was but the figment of a heated brain, developed by his solitary brooding habits. I thought it best to humour him, however, so I quietly asked, "But what will the shepherd say to this course, will he be ready to carry out his part in it ? "

"He'll be com-pelled," replied my uncle grimly, and with this the conversation dropped.

The afternoon wore away while we still continued to sit silently by the stell side, I lamenting that I had ever accepted my uncle's invitation, and making up my mind that the following morning I would depart, my uncle, evidently deep in thought, for occasionally his lips would move and stray words unconsciously escaped him. After we had sat there an hour or more, snow suddenly began to fall, and this at last roused my uncle to action. "Aye," he said to himself, "its snawin', 'twill be a braw neet for a weddin' trip ; come nevvie, 'tis time for us to be gannin'."

It was a long and weary walk home, amidst the eddying snow clouds and the gathering gloom ; twice or thrice I essayed to turn my uncle from the subject which I knew possessed him, but he would not listen, and wearily I trudged alongside, trusting that his mood might change when within doors.

We were about half-a-mile from the cottage when he suddenly broke silence again. "That Airmstrong's a puir fule," he said, "he coorted my wife lang syne, but she'd hae nowt to say to him then when she'd a chance at me. Aye, a puir fule he is, an' at our weddin' when aal the lads were ridin' for the kail, he fell off his horse crossin' the burn, an' was nigh drowned i' the lynn. An' at the "gatherin's" he's aye a muddle-heid, an' nivor kens which is his sheep, and which is na. Man, he tried ance to claim some o' mine, though they were aal marked wiv the " keel," an' a different one to his ain."

I began at last to think that there must be some foundation after all for my uncle's talk ; perhaps an old acquaintance of my aunt's might have dropped in occasionally to ask after her, and show sympathy for her under my uncle's cruel neglect, and it must have been on these slight grounds that my uncle built his suspicions. But now, at last, we were at home again, and breathing a sigh of relief, I shook the snow from my clothes in the doorway, and followed my uncle into the main room beyond. Greatly to my surprise there actually was a man within, sitting in the armchair, by the fireside, opposite to my aunt, and evidently holding converse with her.

My uncle spoke never a word to either as he entered, but I was certain this must be the man of whom he had just been speaking, and an apprehensive feeling as to how the evening would end seized hold upon me. I looked at the man in the armchair, and perceived that he was a handsome looking fellow of some forty years of age, his mouth, however, though somewhat hid by an auburn beard, was weak and drooping, and the glance of his eye, though direct enough, had no force in it. A kind hearted chap, I reflected, but something feeble, and I felt now morally certain that this same individual must be Armstrong, the herd, who had once, according to my uncle, courted my aunt.

Meanwhile my uncle had been busying himself at a drawer in the corner, and was now dragging forth the table from the window, and placing it across the room so as to command the whole interior, and cut off access to the door. I had turned to my aunt, and had not particularly noted my uncle's preparations, when suddenly he called me by name, and looking round I saw that he was seated on the far side of the table with pen, ink, and paper spread before him. Beckoning to me to come close, he whispered excitedly, " I'm gannin' te draw up the writin' I tell't ye of, sit ye doon besides me an' lend a han'."

Alarmed though I was at his manner, for it was evident he was really bent on carrying out his mad intention of the afternoon, I was determined to have no share in his wicked purpose. " I know nothing about it uncle," I replied, " and I'll have no part in it if 'tis what you mentioned on the hill."

" Ding ye for an addle-pate, ye dinna ken either what's releegion nor whilk side your bread's buttered," replied my uncle with such a hard and savage gleam in his eyes that I felt thankful the table was between us. " Nae matter, though," he continued to himself, " I'll manage it çanny, ma lane." With that he fell to scratching upon the papers with his pen, and I turned away and sat down on a stool by my aunt, dumbfounded at the situation.

Meanwhile my aunt and the stranger continued to converse at intervals, and took no notice of my uncle, whose vagaries apparently they had grown accustomed to. Half-an-hour perhaps passed thus in comfortless fashion, when we were roused by a shout from my uncle at the table.

" Stan' up wi' ye, Elinor Crammett, an' Tam Airmstrong, an' listen to what I've written for your eternal behoof." We all stood up together in amazement and looked at one another in perplexity.

" I ken weel," continued my uncle excitedly, his pale blue eyes aflame, and a strange glow of colour on his cheeks, " what's in yor evil hairts, but I'll save ye frae distruction yet, an free masell at the same time frae a fruitless woman. I've written here a writin' o' divorcement agen this woman, for I ken weel her onfaithfulness i' the sperrit, if no' yet i' the body, an' 'tis for ye, Tam Airmstrong, her partner i' the evil thing, to tak' up wi' her an' marry her. Sign the writin' ye maun this night, an' han' in han' pledge each the ither ; then oot ye gan intae the night, an' nivor shew your faces here agen."

My uncle paused, and glared at Armstrong, who was gazing stupified, first at the speaker, and then at the woman beside him. After another moment he spoke, however, and I was surprised at the unexpected courage he displayed."

" Geordie Crammett," he said, " ye ken as weel as I dee that yor wife's as innorcent o' wrang to ye as the babe unborn. Aye, an' ye ken tee dootless that lang syne I courted her, an' she said me nay, an' if sae be as I've leuked in to see her latterly, 'tis but to cheer her up a wee,

for 'tis well kenned ye treat her like a dog.' But noo," he
continued quietly, "if sae be she says she'll gan wi' me,
I'm ready to cherish her as best I may the rest o' my
nattoril life. Will ye gan wi' me, Nell?" he asked, turning
towards the woman beside him as he spoke. "Ay, I'll
gan wi' ye," replied my aunt listlessly, and now for the
first time I realised how broken in spirit she really had
become. "Anything's better than livin' in hell here."

"Sign the writin'," cries my uncle, pointing to the
paper on the table, which he forthwith pushed over
towards Armstrong. The other took the pen in his hand,
subscribed his name, then silently handed it to my aunt,
who did likewise.

"An' noo," continued my uncle afresh, grasp han's,
an' ye woman shall say, 'I'll tak ye for my husband,' an'
ye man, 'I'll tak' ye for ma wife,' then get on yor bonnets
an' be off." The couple silently complied, and in another
moment this strange scene was ended, for without further
speech the newly married man and wife took up, the one
his cap, the other her bonnet and shawl, and hand in hand
moved round the corner of the table, opened the door, and
silently passed out into the night.

"An' wha said I cud na marry them?" shouted my
uncle triumphantly, with a scornful glance at me, "the
meenister hissel cudna hae dyen it cannier, an' noo there's
peace i' the hoose, an' righteousness—an', an', sae te
supper."

With this he proceeded to get eatables out from a
cupboard and spread them on the table, then, having made
fast the outer door, he commenced to make a hearty meal,
beckoning at the same time to me to fall to likewise. "An'
noo," he said suddenly, "we'll hae a muckle great feast the
night, for 'tis a weddin' night, an' there's healths to be
drunk." Rising, he strode to the cupboard again, fetched
therefrom a big green bottle and two glasses, and filling
up both to the brim, seized the nearest, and was about to
toss it off, when a sudden thought seemed to strike him.

"Gosh," he exclaimed in deep dejection, as he put it
down most lothfully, "but I was as nigh as poss'ble
forgettin' 'twas the Sawbath, an' no a day for a carouse.

Ding it aal, but 'tis terr'ble provokin' to be catched by a Sawbath on sich an occasion as this, an' me wi 'a graun thirst on, an' tis three mortal hours till Monday strikes." Glancing at the clock I noticed that it was just on the stroke of nine, and I determined to slip off to bed at once, for I had made up my mind to leave the first thing in the morning. As I lit my candle at the dresser, and bade my uncle good night, I noticed that he was moving about near the clock in a suspicious and uneasy manner, so that out of a curiosity I was moved to stand for a moment in the doorway to see what he was after. Thinking I had gone, he quickly opened the case, rapidly moving the pointers till the clock stood at a quarter to twelve, having done which he heaved a mighty sigh of relief, and I heard him mutter to himself, "It'll no be varry long noo to wait till she strikes Monday, and then,— ma word!"—and he smacked his lips expectantly.

Noiselessly I stole upstairs and reflected with concern upon the strange doings I had just witnessed. The snow had ceased falling, so that there was little chance of the fugitives being lost in the storm before they could find a shelter in a friend's cottage. There was nothing I could do for my unfortunate aunt, so the only purpose I had was to start with daylight and inform my father what had happened.

Just before I fell asleep, I caught the sound of merriment below, and plainly heard my uncle's voice triumphantly uplifting his paraphrase, and dwelling always on the words with ever-thickening emphasis—

"For weel he kenned a woman is
Aye ready for to sin."

'Twas evident, indeed, why my uncle had moved on the clock.

Early next morning I set off, yet not before my uncle had already started with his dogs to look after his sheep, but for this I was not sorry, for any little affection I had previously entertained for him was now turned to aversion, and I could scarce have bidden him farewell with a good grace.

Two days after my return to Jedburgh, news came that

my uncle had been caught in a heavy snowstorm on the hill, as he was returning home from putting his sheep into the " stells," and when searched for next day, had been discovered peacefully lying cold and stiff under a heavy drift of snow.

THE BIGGIN' BY THE LOCH.

ON the western or Scottish side of the Cheviots, at their southern extremity, and a few miles from the Border, the ruins of a small farm, standing above a steep loch side, may still be observed by the stray traveller. The thatch of the roof has long since fallen in, but a trembling rafter here and there seems to show that it must have been inhabited within the memory of man.

No one, however, could now-a-days be found to live there on any condition whatever because of the evil name attaching to it, for it is universally believed to be haunted, and after the fall of twilight the ruin is sedulously avoided by the wayfarer. Certainly no spot more fitted for some desperate deed than this dark and desolate farm-house could ever be imagined. It was a melancholy situation to choose for a human abode. The farm stood alone in its small croft ; behind it rolled away upward the solitary fells, whose short pasturage, cropped by sheep in summer, and in winter bleached by snow and wind, maintained a grey monotony of colour throughout the year, while below, in a deep hollow, the forbidding Dhu Loch lay like a scowl on the landscape's face. Here was the lair, so 'twas fabled, of the great water-bull, whose roaring, on a stormy night, presaged ill for the wayfarer. Beyond the loch a wild moorland stretched away, yet there was good grazing ground attached to the farm some way off down the valley, and in those days the Lamont's, its last inhabitants, were considered, for so poor a district, in the Scotch phrase " responsible " people.

Some forty years ago, Elspeth Lamont and her two sons John and Donald, were living there, and carried on the farm which they rented on easy terms from my uncle. There had always been something strange about Elspeth Lamont ; a strongly marked countenance, deep-set eyes, coal-black hair, a curiously unchanging expression, and a weird lack of colour, gave her an individuality, and impressed the visitor with a feeling of awe it was impossible to shake off. It was well known that she possessed the "second sight," and had on sundry occasions given noteworthy proof of it. Thus at the time of her husband's death, when John and Donald were " but bairns," she had witnessed, as in a distant vision, his final struggle with the storm, and had herself led the way to the spot where, " by the muckle eagle-stane " he was found peacefully lying in the snow. Again, it was she who had found, when all other means had failed, the body of the young Macdonald, who had been drowned in the loch, his boat overturned in a sudden squall. Followed by the relatives of the dead man, she had rowed in her boat to a small creek in the " Fraoch Eileen," and there, beneath the tangle of the drooping branches, had she discovered the corpse. Such, amongst others less significant were the stories John had told me when, long ago, as a school-boy, I first began to fish under his guidance.

John, indeed, was my tutor in all sporting matters, and during the holidays my frequent companion, and gradually I became accustomed on my way back from fishing or shooting to stop at the farm to enquire after their welfare, partake of scones and milk, and enjoy a " crack."

Yet I never could quite get rid myself of a certain dread of Elspeth Lamont ; her weird gift seemed to me to isolate her, as it were, and raise her above the level of ordinary life. A strange sense of personality clung about her at all times, whatever her occupation, and on the occasions of my visits to the farm I always felt, whenever her eyes met mine, that, did she but desire it, she could peer into my soul and handle my secrets as she would.

A few years after her husband's death, things began to go ill at the farm ; John and Donald were now on the eve of manhood, yet Elspeth seemed to believe they were still " bairns," and ruled the household with a rigid hand, feeling doubtless, without her husband, additional responsibility. Donald, the younger son, resembled his father, being of a milder disposition than John, and would be quite content to ply the loom after his day's work was done, or to dream over one of his small stock of books, but John had an obstinate will of his own, loved adventure and sport of all kinds, and rebelled against his mother's stern, though not unkindly rule.

I knew that there was friction in the household, but thought it would pass away, so that when I learnt, some time after my return to school, that John had suddenly left home, the news was a grief as well as a surprise to me.

Next came a report that he was dead, killed, it would seem, in a brawl, though there was, it appeared, but little distinctly known concerning his fate. He had gone up to Edinburgh, it seemed, with his savings in his pocket, and had there fallen in with riotous companions, chief amongst whom (as came out at the examination held later), was a certain profligate sailor, " Three-fingered Jack," for so he was styled owing to his having lost two of the fingers of his right hand in a fight at sea. It further appeared that this same sailor had not only been his constant companion and ill-adviser since his arrival in the town, but was the last individual seen with him on the night of the murder. There was also a rumour as to a girl having in some way or other originated the quarrel, but she too, apparently, had been a stranger in the town and had disappeared some time previously to the murder. In short, nothing definite was known, all was matter of conjecture. No trace could be discovered of the sailor who, it was believed, had shipped himself as extra hand on one of the vessels that left the port of Leith early the next morning.

At all events he had disappeared, and though warrants were issued and search universally instituted, nothing came of it all. Now what made the matter a good deal talked of at the time was the fact (as told me by my uncle in his letters), that Elspeth had witnessed in a vision, as it were, the last tragic scene of her son's life, which vision was looked upon by my uncle, who as " laird " had especially interested himself in the case, as being, though not legally admissable, in itself sufficient evidence to condemn the sailor could he only be brought to justice.

Her vision she described that very night to Donald,

and Donald, next day, in full belief and horror of its truth, had hastened to my uncle, and narrated all the particulars to him. She had seen, she said, John playing at cards in an ill-lit and low ceilinged room with a companion, "a black-a-vised man," as she described him. Both seemingly had been drinking, and a sudden quarrel had sprung up, John striking the stranger in the face. The latter seemed for a moment as if he were about to spring upon his assailant, but drew back a step and spoke some words, as though making an offer of some kind, for he held out his right hand as though to ratify it, and as he did so Elspeth noted the strange fact that his right hand lacked two fingers, the first and second, with startling distinctness, for the maimed outline of his hand was clear against the light of a small lamp burning on the chimney piece. John hesitated, but eventually reached forth his own to take it, then, just as the fingers touched, she saw the stranger whip out with a lightning rapidity his left hand, which he had held concealed behind him, and drive a knife into his companion's heart. Then all became dim, and Elspeth saw no more. The room in which the murder had been committed tallied with Elspeth's description, and it seemed certain, even to the most sceptical, from the fact that the knife was of a foreign workmanship, and had never been seen in Donald's possession, that it was not a case of self-inflicted death but of cowardly murder.

Nothing more could be discovered, however, and gossip, growing weary, soon set off in chase of some fresh quarry.

Of all this I had due information, but it so happened that two years passed away before I again visited my uncle, and in the interval the matter seemed to have faded out of the general remembrance.

The affair, however, had stamped itself upon my memory, and it was one of my first cases to pay the Lamont's a visit. Donald I found much the same, rather quieter of manner than before, perhaps, and less willing to talk than formerly; but Elspeth, on the contrary, had grown more restless, seeming to have lost in part her old self-concentration; there was, too, a curiously eager look about her face that had previously been absent, and, generally, a certain change was noticeable, though it would have been difficult to say exactly wherein it lay.

My visit was but short, however, and I did not see or hear anything of them again until the following year, when I came north again for a stay of some weeks duration. The day after my arrival was wet and stormy, but I determined, nevertheless, to go out for a few hours with my gun to see if I could not pick up a brace or two of grouse or a stray snipe. It chanced after I had been out for an hour or two that I was unfortunate enough, in leaping from one rock to another, to slip and sprain my ankle; to get home was out of the question, and, on reflection, I determined to hobble down as best I could to the Lamont's farm, about three-quarters of a mile distant. Donald would probably be in, and would willingly, I reflected, go up to the house some three miles away and send back a pony for me, so that I might be able to reach home before nightfall.

Making my way painfully along down the rough ground I at last arrived at the farm, and knocking, was at once admitted by Donald. On seeing my condition he volunteered to go up to my uncle's to tell them of my accident and fetch back the pony. As, however, the wind by this time had crept up into half a gale, and the night threatened to be a stormy one, I made him promise, if the weather grew worse, to stay that night at the house, and come back for me early in the morning. Elspeth had offered to shake me down a bed for the night, and I should be perfectly happy, I said, under her care, and without anxiety so long as I knew my uncle's fears at my absence were removed. This he agreed to do, and at once set off along the rough path that led eastward above the waters of the loch. Standing in the door-way, as I said good-night, I marked the wintry aspect of the sky; the wind blew gustily, shivering to pieces the low flying clouds, and beating into anger the waters of the loch below. In the distant sky great piles of cloud were massed of that curious cold and faint-purple colour that betokens snow. Shutting the door I made up my mind at once that I should have to remain there the night, for if the wind went down, a snow-storm was certain. Sitting down on a settle near the fire I watched Elspeth making me up a bed in the corner, for she too was evidently of opinion that I should have to pass the night there. I fell to wondering, idly, how we should "agree," as they say, and whether conversation would be difficult or no, for in times past I had usually addressed my remarks chiefly to John and Donald, having always a nameless awe of her.

I continued to watch her, as, having made the couch ready, she proceeded to prepare materials for a meal ; scones and butter, cold meat and potato, the tea-pot, and the round green whisky bottle, all made their appearance. Not a word did she speak the while, but when all was ready she drew two chairs up to the table, motioned me to one of them, saying as she sat down herself, " Tak ye you ane." Whilst I ate I ventured on some few remarks, with a view to conversation, all of which she wholly ignored, sitting preoccupied, it seemed to me, and listening apparently to the noise of the storm without. On those occasions when a more violent gust than usual tore at the thatch above till the rafters groaned, and the cottage rocked to its very foundations, she would exclaim, as though in answer to herself, " Ay, it's a braw nicht, a braw nicht."

She ate but little herself, but drank sundry cups of tea into which was poured a flavouring of whisky. The meal over, she put away the things, drew up the settle to the ingle-nook for me, threw some fresh peats on to the smouldering ashes of the hearth, then went to the door, and looked forth upon the turmoil outside. I could see through the cracks in the " hallan," that tattered flakes of snow were now driving on the storm, and I knew at once that I should have to remain there the night, for the snow would probably lie inches deep by the morrow's dawn.

Shutting to the door Elspeth shot the bolt, saying as she did so, though apparently to herself, " There's some may be out on the hull the noo wha'd best ha' never left their ain roof-tree the nicht." And now, returning to her chair, she commenced to talk volubly; a suppressed excitement seemed to have taken hold of her; her eyes shone brightly and her hands moved dramatically, illustrating her words. She told me all the news of the country-side, displaying a knowledge I had never credited her with; she asked many questions about my doings at the University, and drew forth my intentions for the future. And all the time I felt somehow that she wished to keep the conversation away from herself, for if ever I ventured to turn it to Donald or herself, she would evade my intention and deftly change the subject to my own doings, or those of my relatives. I would like to have mentioned John's name, and enquired concerning his mysterious fate, and in some way have shewn my sympathy with her, but she feigned to misunderstand, and kept me at arm's length.

An hour or more had passed thus, and it was now about nine o'clock. Sitting there listening to the wailing of the wind without, and marking the play of the firelight upon that stern face, a great fear of her came upon me, an eerie feeling stole over me, and I fell into a reverie. What a strong and absolutely fearless face it was! and what a purpose might lurk in those deep-set, steadfast eyes! Had she lived in the stormier times of the past, how great a part she might have played on the stage of history! The mighty wife of Rob Roy Macgregor had been such another; Flora MacDonald herself would not have surpassed her in fidelity, nor held to a purpose more tenaciously than the woman before me, whose face had iron resolution so clearly stamped upon it.

Thus was I meditating, when suddenly there came a knock on the door outside, and I woke with a start from the world of dreams. Elspeth had gone to the door, and opened it, and now there emerged from the darkness the dim figure of a man, thick set and burly, apparently, and sheeted over with snow. " May be ye'll give me a lodgin' for the night, mistress," said the new-comer, as he strode in without waiting for reply, and commenced stamping upon the floor to divest himself of his snow covering.

" Ay, ye'll be welcome for the nicht," said Elspeth, " ay,
will ye, and a richt Scots welcome will we gie ye the
nicht. Sit ye doun i' the chair by the fire, and warm
yersel'."

There was a curious note of exultation in Elspeth's
voice as she thus bade the stranger so heartily welcome,
and he seemed for a moment a little surprised at her ready
warmth, but he sat down at once by the fire, thanking her
kindly, and heaved a sigh of relief as he stretched forth his
legs over the warm peats.

" Its a fearful night," he said, addressing himself
to me, for Elspeth was now busy getting out the relics
of our supper for the stranger's refreshment. " Bein' out
on such a night as this," he continued, " might make one
think almost, if one had an ill conscience, that the wind and
snow had a purpose to destroy one; whenever I came
anigh the edge of the path, down swooped the wind,
draggin' me, as it were, to the brink, and strivin', tooth
and nail, to thrust me into the lake, while the snow
blinded the eyes, fair dazzlin' me. Many's the dirty night
I've passed at sea, but never one so dirty as this."

" Ay, 'twas gay and lucky ye fun' the hous," replied
Elspeth, who had overheard his words, " an' folk to
welcome ye; it was the hand of Providence may be,"
and again the same strange tone of exultation sounded
in her voice, ringing clearly as a bell above the noise
of the storm. " And noo," she continued, " if ye're
warmed eneuch, there's a bit supper for ye," pointing to
the table, " turn the chair roon, and ha'p yersel'."

" Thank-ye," said the stranger, " thank-ye, I'm half
clemmed with hunger, not havin' had bite nor sup since
leavin' Heatherton at twelve this mornin'." So saying, he
fell to ravenously, while Elspeth continued to move around
him, seeing all his wants were provided for.

The stranger was evidently a sea-faring man, his talk
had indicated so much, and his clothes gave confirmation.
Dressed in blue broadcloth, and wearing a heavy pilot coat,
he had the appearance of a merchant sailor of the better
class; he was of medium stature and thick-set, and, from
what I could gather from his free and easy air, his jaunty

carriage, his dark bronzed face, marked here and there with a scar, he seemed one of the reckless, dare-devil sort.

He soon demolished what had been set before him; then filled an inch long cutty pipe with tobacco, and emptying the contents of the round green bottle into a big tumbler, thrust his chair nearer the fire, and filling up with hot water from the kettle, sipped his mixture contentedly, and drawing deep breaths of tobacco smoke, commenced to talk in the egotistic manner of a sailor.

"Mebbe, ye'll be wunderin' how 'tis I come to be wanderin' about in these desolate parts, and me a seafaring man," he commenced, "but bless ye, I've been everywhere, high and low, far and near, in my time; beginning life in a sea-port town, I served the sea for my 'prenticeship, did a bit of smugglin' at one time when the world was easier than 'tis now, digged gold in Australee, kept a bar for a while in Melbourne, but bein' a ungentlemanly trade, chucked that and took to the sea agen, and now I'm purposed to swing at anchor the rest o' my days, with a tender-ship alongside o' me, d'ye see?" Here he laughed loudly and winked at me, then in reply to a question from myself, explained himself further. "This is how 'tis—' but three years ago I was in Edinburgh, bein' paid off after a longish voyage, an' I fell in there with a han'some lass, a strong upstandin' gal, a canny lass that knew a man when she saw one, an' could reckon his vally. Well, I just lost no time, ye may tak' your davy o' that, an' the upshot was that if I came back, after another voyage, with a bit o' brass saved, she'd splice me, if so be she'd not found a properer man in the meantime. Well, off she goes to Lunnon to take service there for a while, leavin' me to finish my carouse 'long shore afore shipping agen to collec' the brass agen the weddin' day.'" Here he paused to take up his glass, and having drained the tumbler to the dregs, proclaimed in arrogant tones: "There's Janet's health, and never a better toast in the kingdom. She'd lines to catch a man's eye amid a crowd of other sail, and happy the man who can call himself skipper of such a craft!" The whisky had evidently had its influence upon him, his face had become more flushed,

his manner noisier, and his tongue more garrulous than
before.

"Ay, she was well worth fighting for was Janet," he
continued, "an' sad it was to leave her at a moment's
notice, but 'twas necessary, as it chanced, and, bein'
hurried like, as I may say, there was no choice but to take
third mate's place on board an old sea-coffin of a brig
whose sailing orders were ready, bound for Mexico; an'
'twas little I ever expected to fetch harbour, but we'd a
rare passage, an' with the brass I had over I made a
tolerable lucky venture out there; so here I am back
again wi' a fair warm linin' for a stockin'—here he tapped
his chest pocket significantly, and continued vivaciously—
"Ay, an' mebbe in three weeks time there'll be one able-
bodied seaman the less, an one fam'ly man the more, for
Janet's still single, an' I've a letter from her to say she's ready
for the job.—I'd an address in Lunnon ye see, where I got
news of her as soon as ever I landed, an wrote her at onst.
She'd been back i' these parts somewhile it seemed, an'
bein' an orphan does the housekeeping for an uncle, a
shepherd, that's livin' on the hills about 10 mile from here.
T'was there I was steerin' a straight course for, by
compass across the moor, when the storm came on, an' I
was forced to lay to, an' was lucky enough to find such
friendly folk as mistress here."

His story ended, he stooped down to the hearth, and
knocked the ashes carefully out of his pipe—and as he did
so I suddenly saw, plain against the glow of the peat, that
two fingers of his right hand were missing. Startled out
of my self control by the strange sight, an involuntary cry
escaped me—surely this same stranger could be none
other than "Three-fingered Jack" of the murder. The
suggestion came in a flash, everything seeming to tally;
but the sailor had now turned to me asking what ailed me,
and at the same moment I caught a glimpse of Elspeth's
face, her eyes, it seemed to me in my terror, full of an
indescribable look demanding my inmost thoughts.
Endeavouring to collect myself, and grasping the frightful
nature of the situation, I made a mighty effort for self-
control, and stammered out that my ankle had given a

sudden twinge and forced me to cry out. " Ay," said
Elspeth, rising, " the young laird's lame the nicht, an' will
be glad to sleep, an ye'll be tired too maybe, an' ready
eneuch for bed. Ye can just hae Donald's room the nicht,
for he's awa an' will not be back till the morn. 'Tis lucky
he's awa the nicht, ay, an ye're lucky as said the noo, ye
that hae a fine lass awaitin' ye the morn."   Thus speaking
Elspeth strode to the dresser to light the candles, and as
she turned again towards us I marked her pride of gait,
her resolute aspect, her glowing eye, and a great awe took
hold upon me.

   " Sleep ye well," she said to me, and in her voice
sounded yet more strongly, I fancied, that same note of
exultation I had noticed previously.   " Gang ye up first,"
said Elspeth to the sailor, handing him a lighted candle,
and motioning him to the stair. She took up the other
herself, and mounted after him.   I watched them breathlessly, the sailor mounting light-heartedly, humming the
fragment of some sea ditty ; Elspeth following hard behind
him, stern and silent, rigid as fate.   At the top they
parted, he to the left to Donald's room, she to the right to
her own.

   I heard the sailor shut his door and shoot the bolt,
then Elspeth entered her own room, and hearing her move
about the small chamber above my head, I drew breath
again with a mighty sense of relief.

   I could not have told what I expected, but some terrible
deed seemed imminent, and now that the unsuspecting
sailor was safely housed behind his bolted door my nervous
tension was somewhat lightened, and I could, with some
approach to calmness, think over the situation.   I never
for a moment doubted that this sailor was "Three fingered
Jack," after whom my uncle had made search at the time
of the examination, the presumable murderer of poor John,
and the " black-a-vised man " of Elspeth's vision. Everything fitted in with the supposition ; the sailor's own easy
confessions, his presence in Edinburgh at that time, the
rumour about a lass being mixed up with the quarrel, and
lastly, what bore, of course, greatest weight of all, the
startling evidence of the two first fingers of his right hand

being absent. I wondered how it was I had not sooner noticed this, but the light was dim, and now that I thought about it, he seemed indeed always to have used his left hand for anything he wished to do. Had Elspeth noticed it too? This was the question that now filled my mind to the exclusion of all other thoughts.

No, upon a calmer reflection I concluded she had not, for she had kept silence all the time the stranger had been narrating his history, and I remembered to have thought she had even fallen asleep. Even when at the moment of my discovery, I had uttered that foolish cry, I remembered now that her face had been turned towards the firelight and away from the sailor, and that when she had turned upon me with that strange gaze, her face had worn no other expression than that of stern enquiry.

There was now no sound from above, both Elspeth and the sailor having apparently fallen asleep, and quieter thoughts stole into my mind. Quickly I made my plans. Next morning at day's dawn I would hobble off and inform my uncle of my discovery, and he of course would forthwith take steps to secure this same three-fingered Jack, who was, I could not doubt, poor John's assassin.

Though such thoughts as these brought comfort with them, I yet resolved that there was one thing still to be done before I could lay aside my fears and compose myself to sleep, and that was to discover, by actual investigation, whether the sailor had really shot his bolt and so secured his safety for the night.

Cautiously, then, I rose, and hobbled towards the stairs, and mounting them with infinite difficulty and pain, on hand and knee I finally gained the top, reached out my hand and found the door of the sailor's room, which I pressed with outstretched hand. I rejoiced when I found it firmly fixed, not yielding in the least to my pressure ; then I slowly descended, with a mind tolerably at ease, and placing myself on the couch fell instantly to sleep, tired out with all that had happened that day.

I slept soundly at first, but gradually terrible fancies ruffled the placid surface of sleep. Confused and misty images floated across my brain, but gradually a space

cleared, and I saw, as in a vision, two flying figures, the
one pursuing, the other fleeing, as if for life. The pursuer
was gaining quickly on the pursued, and now they were
close upon me, and I saw that the hunter was Elspeth,
the fugitive the sailor. Then I perceived a third
figure blocking the path in front of the sailor, in whose
angry lineaments I recognized the features of the dead
John. A fearful shriek seemed to fill the air around me,
and I woke to find a deathly stillness prevailing in the
house, and saw the pale moonbeams streaming in through
the windows with faint and ghostly light. Reassured at
finding everything so quiet I endeavoured once more to
calm the agitation of my mind, when suddenly there broke
upon the stillness what seemed the weird moaning of a hound.
I quaked upon my bed, as I sat upright listening to the
sound, remembering the superstition of the Highlands,
which avers 'tis the tolling for a departed soul. Then I
recollected the existence of my retriever, who had been
shut up in the lean-to at the back of the house, and this
thought brought some comfort to my mind. Still, I was
so unnerved I felt I could not remain inactive. I looked
at my watch and found it was three o'clock, still two hours
at least before I could hope to get away.

To quieten my uneasiness I determined once more to
ascend the stairs and make trial of the door, to ascertain if
it was still fast as before. Still more cautiously and
laboriously than before I mounted, rested at the summit to
gain my breath, stretched out my hand again—and lo!
to my horror this time I found the door gave way to my
pressure, slight as it was.

A great fear seized me—an electric sense of some
horrible thing took hold of me, and I could scarce keep
myself from a fainting fit. Summoning up all my courage,
I rose desperately to my feet, thrust open the door, and
there before my eyes gleamed, livid in the moonlight, the
upturned face of the sailor, a ghastly grin upon his
countenance, his lips drawn back and his white teeth
glistening savagely in the ghostly moonlight.

In that one moment I knew he was dead—no living
face could have looked like that—and I reeled back against

the door post, my mind whirling like a top, everything swimming before my eyes. Gradually I recovered my consciousness, and my eyes sought again that dreadful countenance, and though I loathed to look, I could not help but gaze. Drawing involuntarily a step nearer, I plainly saw the thin stream of blood that marked his flannel shirt; his coat and waistcoat were wide open, and there, standing straight up from his chest, dark in the moonlight, rose the handle of a dirk I had once, long ago, given to the departed John.

Sick at heart, I tottered out of the room, and, scarce knowing what I did, turned to the chamber opposite and looked within for Elspeth. No one was there; the moon's rays lit the room; the bed clothes were still unturned. I raised my voice and cried " Elspeth, Elspeth." No answer came save only the howling of the dog below. I could not stay another moment in that house of death, so turning, I fled hastily down stairs, and forgetting my lame ankle, undid the latch and bolt, and rushed forth into the night.

Not much now remains to tell, nor in fact could I relate how painfully I struggled those long three miles through the deep snow-drifts, and finally arrived at my uncle's house.

All I remember is that I had just strength sufficient to rouse the still sleeping inmates, when I sank upon the door-step. When I awoke to consciousness it was broad daylight; men had been sent to the cottage and these found all as I had left it, and the dead man the sole inmate of the house. Footsteps were found in the snow leading down to the loch, and as Elspeth was never seen again in this world, it was believed that, her vengeance accomplished for which alone she had lived, she had found a quiet grave beneath the dark waters of the loch.

Enquiry, of course, was held, and I gave my evidence, and was duly exonorated of whatever shadow of suspicion might have fallen upon me; and though sometimes I feel inclined to blame myself for my inaction, the universal belief held by people in those parts comforts my conscience, which avers that throughout the hand of Providence was plainly visible.

As for Donald, he was quite shattered by this last blow that had fallen upon his house, and went about like a broken man, and as soon as the magisterial enquiry was ended emigrated over the seas to begin life anew. He came to see me to say good-bye, and the last words I ever heard him speak were these : "Good-bye sir," he said, "and thank ye again and again for your kindness to me and to them that's gone, and, sir," he continued in a faltering voice, "dinna ye think too ill o' my mither, for she was sorely temptit ; she lo'ed John like the apple o' her ee, an' aye blamed hersel' for the quarrel that drave him frae the door, though there was blame o' bath sides, as I may say. Ay, sir, an' it's my belief she jest lived to do her vengeance, fore seein' wi' her gifts that ae day the murderer wad come to her very door-cheek, pittin' his life in her han's. Wi' a temptation sic as that ye'll no be blamin' her over mickle mebbe, an' whiles, though the meenister micht say 'twas papistical, I just offer up a bit prayer for her soul."

Thus Donald spoke and said good-bye . . . . . Such then is the story the passing stranger will be told if he enquire why the "biggin'" by the Dhu Loch's side is crumbling to ruins, and is now almost level with the ground.

THE ELDER OF NORTH QUAY.

THE town of North Quay lies on the farther side of a certain important river in the North of England, and was once well known to sailors all the seas over, owing to its proximity to the river's mouth, and to the fact that vessels frequently unloaded there and sought repairs in the various dry docks and yards, from whence arose a constant clatter of rivetters and platers at their work. Now, however, it is much less busy than formerly, owing to the competition of a new port on the southern side of the river.

Thus it had gradually attained to an antique and picturesque appearance; sundry warehouses, for example, had fallen into decay on the river's bank, and at low tide showed black misshapen limbs, on which the green seaweeds, like an evil disease, festered in spots.

The houses rose up tier above tier, from the very brink of the river to the full height of the hill behind, red-tiled for the most part, with curious tall and crooked chimneystacks that reminded the stranger of a foreign town; here and there a gable end had fallen in, and the irregular outline of its ruin added to the general effect of the whole.

Down by the quayside, and along the lower length of the town, ran a curiously narrow and curving road, that but barely admitted the passage of a cart.

All the length of this thoroughfare was crowded with public-houses and drinking booths: here and there, indeed, a marine store displayed a dingy window stuffed with ancient clothes, offering facilities for re-opening a credit next door; nor were there wanting sundry chandlers' shops, from whose doors a pungent odour was emitted. Occasionally the signs of other trades also might be seen: enormous painted boots hung high in air, and on a windy day were a frequent source of alarm to the passers-by;

F

sundry inscribed **boards** proclaimed that up the various alleys that **opened on** to the roadway travellers might be housed for **the night as cheaply as the** good Samaritan lodged his *protégé*. But the **public-houses so** greatly **predominated, and were** there **indeed in such** numbers, **that a certain well-known character in the town,** of **proved capacity, had refused to back himself to walk** down **the length of it, take a glass at each, and pronounce his own name at the other end.**

There were, **however, as was but natural, one or two of** these places of **resort** more popular **than the rest,** notably " **The Spotted Dog** " **and** " The Goat in Boots," where custom **and a reputed** easiness in the landlord had **founded** a **reputation.** The last named inn was **the** favourite resort **of merchant sailors,** and **stood** in the **centre of the narrow street, a little** back from the pavement ; in front **stood a tall mast from** which swung a signboard, whereon a **fantastic creature in** large sea-boots was understood—by **the artist at all** events—to **be capering** vivaciously.

One night towards the **close of** November, ten **years** ago, it chanced that the " **Goat in Boots** " was unusually **crowded. A large East Indiaman had just come** in, and **the inhabitants of the town, relishing a now rare** honour, **had come in force to see the strangers** and hear the stories **they would surely be willing to tell.**

In the taproom a **bright fire blazed, calling** forth a **responsive gleam from the dark panelling that ran round the room. The floor was clean and sanded, the** long **tables resounded with the clink of pewter and the ring** of glasses, **and the atmosphere was thick with laughter and** tobacco smoke.

Round **the chimney corner, and** lounging in the **armchairs provided for superior guests,** were two or three of **the new comers, whose words** were reverently listened to **by the** *habitués* **of the place, whose** knowledge of naval **matters, though great, was essentially theoretical.** Nearer **the door sat a swarthy seaman, gay with** bright coloured **neck-cloth, rings in his ears and on** his fingers, who **was earnestly endeavouring,** notwithstanding occasional **hiccoughs, to convince his neighbour—a** timid shoemaker from next door—of the dangers of the deep and the better security of terra firma. Quite close to the entrance was a nondescript group, consisting generally of those who hoped to scrape acquaintance with the new arrivals, and, by learning their weaknesses, to glean advantages for themselves; amongst whom touts—that one-eyed, errand-running race of men—and red-faced, Amazonian females, who might fitly have lectured on the equality of the sexes, were plainly visible.

In the middle of the room, and at a table by himself, sat a tall, white-haired, venerable old man, who looked superior to, and yet quite at his ease among his strange companions. He might have been observed to be taking secret note of all that was going on out of the corner of his half-shut eyes; yet, though his eyes were thus apparently only half open, his glance was clear and keen as a hawk's, and the paper he held in his hands was merely a pretext for escaping observation and avoiding conversation. One figure more especially occupied his, as well as the general attention—that, namely, of a stranger who was sitting in the corner nearest the fire in the chief place, with a wise-looking parrot on his shoulder and a big cheroot between his lips.

Stories of adventure had been freely circulating amidst a din of laughter, applause, and the clink of pewter, but when the owner of the parrot spoke, his individuality seemed to assert itself, for the noise gradually ceased and the space of silence about him gradually widened.

He was certainly of interesting appearance: his hair was long and hung in curls about his shoulders; his face, through exposure to the sun, was of a dark tan hue, while his eyes were of the deep blue colour that typifies the sea on a summer day, and is only to be found amongst the race of sailors. His hands and arms were tattooed with quaint symbols and devices, and in the lines of his mouth was visible a humourous expression, which, taken in connection with his easy attitudes, gave him the air of one who has seen the world and found it to his liking.

There seemed, indeed, to cling about him a scent of romance and adventure: a Sindbad of the nineteenth century, imagination whispered, plucking, as he spoke, expectation's sleeve.

Some of the bystanders had remarked upon the strange colouring and wise aspect of the parrot that sat upon his shoulder and surveyed the company with cold penetrative eyes.

" Ay, ay," said he, in response to some query, " she's a wise bird, yon is, and knows more than many a human. The Indian priest who gave her me said she was more nor fifty years old, and a curious history it was that he told of her.   He believed there was a spirit inside of her.   She was always findin' out things he'd have rather kept hid, and had a memory for them that was quite as perplexin' as it was disgustin', so he said.   Ay, ay," continued the sailor, stroking the parrot's head, " there's many a queer yarn she could tell ye had she a mind to, but she just holds her tongue and laughs at the folly of other people."

Here one of the bystanders, charmed by this description, endeavoured to conciliate the wise but cynical bird by also stroking her head.   She, however, resenting the impertinence, caught him by the forefinger and tweaked it so sharply that the blood was visible.   Roars of laughter followed this reverse, whilst the unfortunate individual uttered hearty imprecations, to which the parrot listened intently, but not finding any fresh additions therein to her own vocabulary, proceeded to shut her eyes in scornful manner and go to sleep.

" Ay, mates," began the sailor again, when the merriment had subsided, " she could tell ye, had she a mind to do so, queer things enough, but as she won't, why, I'll tell ye a yarn myself about how this jewel came into my possession," drawing, as he spoke a little green case forth from the inner pocket of his red-lined pilot coat, which he placed on the table in front of him.   Then slowly opening it, he disclosed to the wondering gaze of the spectators a magnificent pearl, which, for size, purity, and lustre, far surpassed any to be seen in the richest jewellers' windows.

" It shines like a lamp, mates," he continued, amidst the hum and rustle of admiration, holding it up between his fingers that its sheen might be the more apparent.

"'Twas an heirloom, as the great folks say, and has a history as long as my arm, I'll warrant ye, though I can only tell ye how it came to be in my possession. 'Tis about a year or more agone that I was aboard the 'Nizam', outward bound for the East Indies. We'd put into Constantinople, however, to discharge freight and take in coal, and finding the time hanging heavy on my hands, I wandered about a bit one day to see the place. Well, I was tacking about up and down the main streets, trying to catch a glimpse of the ladies under their veils, which they wear, I b'lieve, to prevent their bein' found out. 'Taint in women's nature, d'ye see, to wear a veil if so be they're handsome. I was just returnin' to the ship then, when all of a sudden clap comes a hand on my back, and turnin' round, whom did I see but the young Squire, on whose place I had been brought up at home.

" ' Jack ! ' says he, quite astonished, 'who'd ha' thought of seein' you here ? Why, its Fate,' says he. ' Kismet, sure enough, as they say out here. You're just the very man I want, so come along with me,' says he, ' and I'll tell ye all about it,' clappin' his arm through mine and halin' me along like a p'liceman, takes me to his hotel.

" Well, dashed if it warn't just one of them Turkish women I'd just been sneerin' at ! The young Squire had been travellin', d'ye see, makin' a 'grand tour ' as he called it, to complete his eddication : eddication not bein' complete, of course, without a lesson or two from the fair sex." Here the narrator paused a moment, gave a mighty wink at a nervous-looking little man near him, drained his glass, and continued with a smile :

" He'd made up his mind to marry her there and then, run the blockage, and carry her off if need were. There was need enough and to spare indeed, for her Pa, d'ye see, was a minister, a Pasha, they called him ; a hooked nose, fiery Turk, who hated Christians, and more especially Englishmen, like pork, which those pagunds say is unclean, though they ain't over-clean themselves, if it comes to that. Well, notwithstanding all this, and all I could say against it—and I was strong against it, too, tellin' him as how he was over-young for the job, and could take his choice in

England when the proper time came—' Why,' says I, forgetting myself for the moment, ' as for runnin' away with a foreign gal in a veil—why, it's like buyin' a pig in a poke.'

" ' Jack,' says he, laughin' quite in a good humour at the notion, as it were, ' you'll be ready to eat your foolish words when once you've seen her.' Well, I didn't think so, but I said no more, seein' the uselessness of it, for 'tis the skipper pricks the chart and the seaman must just obey.

" So I agreed to be at a certain point that night at eleven o'clock and follow out all his instructions, happen what might. Well, I might ha' been seen that night, at the very moment the clock was strikin' ten, clamberin' up a great high wall that shut in the Nabob's paliss and grounds.

" I'd to wait, d'ye see, just below the wall, in the shadow of a fig-tree, for her to come, then help her over the wall by a rope ladder I had round my waist, and jump into the carriage which was to be there ready for us—the young Squire himself bein' the cabby, dressed out in linen togs and turban to distract attention.

" 'Twas a nasty wall to climb, was yon : I doubt if I hadn't been a sailor I'd never ha' got to the top ; however, I managed after a bit to get a foothold, and swingin' myself up to the top, lay there to get my breath. First thing I see is a great scowling sentry just below me with a nasty heathen sword like a sickle waiting for me. There wasn't a moment to think about anything at all—I just made a jump on to him there and then—almost fell on him, in fack, and by good luck stunned him as I came down pretty heavy right on top of him. I was mighty pleased it was him that was stunned and not me, as there'd ha' been mighty little chance of my ever seein' the light again, had he had a say in the matter. For fear, however, he might come to before the young lady was to arrive I took the turban off his head and tied it tight round his mouth like a gag, and then, tying his hands behind his back, left curlytoes senseless on the grass and hid myself in the shade of the fig-tree. Two or three minutes passed away, and I trembled at every sound, fearing lest an alarm had been given and it was all up. Yet all of a sudden comes a rustling noise, and, lo and behold, there she was! Well, mates, she was just like——"

Here the narrator's imagination, proving unequal to the task, sought a stimulus in the glass that had been judiciously ordered by one of the audience beforehand and placed beside him.

" Ay, ay," continued the sailor slowly, "its no use talkin', but she beat a fairy in a pantomime hollow—a bit pale, perhaps, she was, but her eyes shone like stars on a clear night in the Indian Seas, glimmerin' as 'twere, with grace and beauty, like the pearl ye've seen to-night.

" Well, it wasn't many minutes before she was over that blessed wall and safe into the carriage t'other side. Off we drove to the hotel, and there that very evening they were married by an English clergyman who happened to be out there at the time. Ay! married right enough, no doubt about that : why, I gave her away myself and witnessed their signatures, ay, and got a kiss too for the job, and what I valued less at the time, mates, this here pearl as well," again producing it as he spoke from his pocket.

" No, no," cried the honest sailor in conclusion, "he promised true enough to love and to cherish her till death did them part, else, squire or no squire, he'd not ha' had my help ! "

A murmur of applause greeted this manly and essentially British sentiment that so fitly brought the tale to a conclusion.

The story of the pearl had monopolised all attention, and the men gazed reverently upon the possessor of a jewel that had been so romantically won. Polite attentions were plentifully shown the honest sailor, offers of "something hot" resounded on all sides of him, but now mine host came forward and intimated, with deprecating smile and finger pointed to the clock, that the time had come when he, however unwillingly, was forced to close his doors and frown upon festivity.

The company slowly broke up and dispersed in little groups of twos and threes, all discussing the sailor and his pearl and repeating again the romantic details of its history.

The venerable looking individual who, as was noticed above, had taken such an interest in all that was going on, though he had not joined in the throng of those who offered their services, was awaiting with impatience an opportunity of accosting the possessor of this priceless jewel. "Good-nights" were exchanged outside as the company broke up and went their various ways, and the sailor, who had refused all the invitations for prolonging the night that had been showered upon him, was left standing alone for a moment in the middle of the street.

The venerable old man, perceiving his opportunity, came up at once and thus accosted him.

"My friend," said he, "if I may without offence thus style a stranger, should it so happen that you seek a lodging I offer my humble roof to your notice."

Here he produced a card on which was inscribed in large letters—

EBENEZER STALLYBRASS,

6, Marine Terrace.

FURNISHED APARTMENTS.

which he impressively handed over to the sailor.

"Ay," he continued slowly, "at 6, Marine Terrace, I, Ebenezer Stallybrass, let lodgings ; charges moderate, all things cleanly and orderly, and an extraordinary fine prospect of the sea, which will be very pleasing to a sailor." "Ay," he commenced again after a moment's pause, "and lest ye should fear ye might be robbed I may tell ye that I am an Elder o' the Kirk and well respecked in the town."

"Ay," he concluded, after another and most impressive pause, during which the sailor had difficulty in subduing a smile, "at 6, Marine Terrace there's prayers morning and evening and all the comforts of a home."

It may be doubted whether the honest sailor would have included prayers in the category of home comforts, but at all events he seemed impressed by what he heard, or perhaps it was rather that he was amused by the manners and character of his would-be host, for he reflected for a short space, and a humorous twinkle lit up

his eye as he replied, " Well, thank ye, mate, I've got a
berth for to-night, but I'll look ye up to-morrow, and
maybe I'll stay with ye a bit, though as to prayers, now,—
well, I'm one who's for prayer myself—but——"

" Ay, ay," interrupted the other quickly, " prayers are
no compulsory, but, eh mon ! ye'll just have been tarr'bly
neglecked at sea—the main part of ye.   Ay, 'twill be just a
gran' opportunity for ye if ye lodge with me."

The mariner laughed good-humouredly, amused as a
prosperous man may be when sympathised with for a loss
he does not feel, then turning away with a hearty good-
night, walked off down the street.   He had not gone very
far, however, before he felt a tap upon his shoulder, and,
looking quickly round, perceived the venerable Elder, who
again accosted him.   " Friend," he said, " I'm no one of
those that lightly speak evil of my neighbours, but I'm
thinkin' it's the plain duty of one man to another to warn
ye that there's some here who would rob ye a'most for the
price of a glass of whisky."

" Ay," he continued, solemnly, " and wi' a pearl like
yon upon ye it would be a sin no to tak' precautions.
Now, if ye would like to deposit it wi' me for the night I'll
take the risk wi' it, and I'll gie ye a receipt for it the
while," said he, taking as he spoke a book from his pocket,
and carefully wetting a pencil between his teeth, prepared
to save his neighbours from temptation.

" It's all right with me, thank ye kindly," replied the
sailor, amused at the other's warning and anxiety to
bestow the pearl in a place of security.   " No, no," he
continued, " you reckon I can pretty well steer a right
course by this time, fair weather or foul ! "   With this he
moved away again, leaving Ebenezer standing still with
his book open in his hand, watching his retreating figure
with anxious eyes and fearful for his safety.

As the honest mariner made his way homeward he
might have been heard to laugh again and again at the
thought of his would-be landlord.   Though he had seen,
like a certain famous traveller of old, " the manners and
cities of men," he had not lost his native simplicity or been
taught to distrust his neighbour ; nay, his travels had

quickened his human interest, and led him to take new interest in every fresh type of character he encountered. He had now, indeed, almost made up his mind to lodge at the house of the Elder, whereas a more cautious man would probably have hesitated to face such a formidable combination of qualities as went to make up Ebenezer's personality.

The honest mariner dimly guessed indeed that Ebenezer was a complex character, but he did not endeavour to form any analysis, but came to the simple conclusion that "Scottie" was a rum customer, and from that fact promised himself some amusement.

The honest mariner, however, as we said above, troubled himself not about these things, but next day betook himself to Marine Terrace in order to inspect Ebenezer's apartments. He found them much to his liking and fully bearing out, so far as he could see, the description given of them. Not merely were the rooms neat and simple, and commanded a good prospect of the sea, but a pretty parlour maid answered the bell, as it turned out, and added another attraction which was "very pleasin' to a sailor." It was this, perhaps, rather than the situation, or the fact that his landlord was an original, or even the rusty telescope in the garden, as large as a small cannon, of which he could have the gratuitous use, that clinched his desire and determined him to have his chest brought up thither at once.

The next few days passed by pleasantly enough, the sailor thought, as he peaceably smoked his pipe in the garden on a warm afternoon, and in the evening sat in his arm-chair beside the red-bricked fireplace, where a fire always burned cheerily, keeping the hobs—those brackets so convenient for after-dinner enjoyment—warm and ready for their uses.

As for the "prayers—morning and evening" the honest sailor had devoutly attended at first, and had somewhat disconcerted Ebenezer—who previously had always been listened to by the two servants in perfect silence—by uttering devout, but unfortunately ill-timed, amens : as for example, when Ebenezer paused to take in a fresh supply of breath. What had finally put an end to the sailor's attendance was not the "prayer" so much as the "exposeetion," as Ebenezer called it, which followed, wherein he sustained the part of "devil's advocate" with efficacy, exposing the weak side of various apostles and divines with an unfailing satisfaction.

"Ay," he remarked one evening in an "exposeetion," suggested by a chapter he had just read from one of the Epistles, "ay, St. Paul, now, had a gran' eloquence, doubtless, and a choice of words quite extraordinary, but he was aye over-weak in doctrine—whiles beseeching instead of threatening, and aye leaving the sinner a loophole for escape. Ye cannot coax the sinner to righteousness wi' a kiss, but wi' threats maun drive him afore ye as an auld wife brings hame her kye of an evening. 'Twas a greet peety, too, he should write of himself as bein' weak in bodily presence, and in speech contemptible.' Ay, 'twas a peety, indeed, he should ha' been so meek—ay, and a sair peety that others who ha' the gifts should lack the opportuneeties." .

Then there ensued an impressive pause which was broken unexpectedly by the sailor, who, but dimly understanding what had been said, and believing something to be expected from him, audibly ejaculated "Amen!" and thereby so startled the elder that some of the hard sayings destined for another fell upon himself.

After this the sailor no longer attended prayers, notwithstanding the expostulations of the landlord, who enlarged upon the "building up" the "exposeetion" never failed to effect.

To this he bluntly replied that "there wasn't no chance for one of the crew if the skipper were trounced like that," alluding to the above-mentioned attacks on the divines of old. .

Indeed, he more than suspected that Ebenezer's scheme of righteousness worked out in the form of an equation, whereby the election of one just man, viz., Ebenezer, was equivalent to the rejection of ninety-and-nine unjust persons, amongst whom the sailor felt he was himself included.

He dimly guessed, indeed, that his future host combined several diverse qualities in his constitution, and, had he been gifted with the analytical spirit, he might have likened him to a prodigy of old, an instance of the "triformis" class, composed of three very different elements, of which elements, the Scot would generally predominate, assisted by the second—the lodging-house keeper—while on Sundays of course the Elder would reign supreme. It might be surmised, moreover, that on the remaining six days of the week the elements of the Scot and the lodging-house keeper—when any mutual advantage was obtainable—would be only too ready to lay violent hands upon the unfortunate Elder and incontinently imprison him.

He had discovered very soon that it was not so much the desire to save him from destruction, as the extraordinary affection he had for his pearl, that had made Ebenezer so eager to secure him as a lodger.

For every evening after the Bible had been put away his landlord would come downstairs, and under pretence of seeing that his guest was comfortable, would enter into conversation and sit down opposite him. Before he departed, the conversation would be sure to turn sooner or later to the wonderful pearl; the story of course resulted, and finally, in answer to certain hints, the pearl itself would be drawn from its case, to prove, as it were, the authenticity of the story.

The sailor, indeed, was nothing loath to tell the romantic history as often as might be, but yet found mighty satisfaction in pretending not to notice Ebenezer's hints that came fluttering forth each evening after prayers, like bats or moths about a lamp, as he used to slily reflect within himself.

Many were the groans Ebenezer had to give vent to before his hints would be perceived by his obtuse lodger, whose insensibility invariably increased as the eagerness of the other was more openly displayed. The period of suspense was prolonged, in fact, each evening, till, as the sailor used to mischievously describe it, " it wasn't afore he had burnt both wings and was buzzin' about and around the pearl like a bluebottle fly," that the torture was ended by its production.

Here, indeed, the sailor felt he had his host at a disadvantage, and could repay with interest on the material side some of the severe buffets he had himself received in the spiritual discipline he had been subjected to.

On one occasion, indeed, he even went so far as to pretend he had lost it, and Ebenezer's face worked like that of a man in a fit. Indeed his passion for the pearl was fast consuming him, and with his passion his hate of the owner of the pearl grew correspondingly, not, of course, because he envied him a mere carnal possession, but that his spiritual pride was wounded at thus having to ask a favour of one who was a mere castaway.

Matters, however, came to a crisis one evening. It so happened that Ebenezer had been reading at prayers that night concerning the merchant in the bible who sold all his possessions in order to buy a pearl of great price. The incident thus recorded had taken immediate hold of his imagination, for the merchant, it seemed to him, had been in a similar position to that wherein he himself was placed at the moment. The question that at once occupied him was the amount of the sum thus raised by the merchant that proved sufficient for the purpose.

" Could it have been as much as £500 ? " cogitated Ebenezer, as he slowly descended the stairs, groaning within himself the while at the immensity of the amount.

He found his lodger at home, as was usual in the evening, and after a few preliminary and inconsequent remarks skilfully, as was his wont, led up to the great subject. When again the jewel was disclosed, he could restrain himself no longer, but was fain to discover once for all—though several times previously he had thrown out judicious feelers on the subject—whether his lodger would be willing to part with it—at a price.

" May be," he questioned insidiously—" ye can give a guess as to what the value of it might be," peering out as he spoke, from under his bushy eye-brows at his careless lodger who sat in the arm-chair opposite.

" Oh ! I dessay a thousand pounds, maybe," replied the other in his offhand way.

" Eh ! a thousand pounds ! " echoed the horror-struck Ebenezer. " Man ! ye can never mean it. Na, na, you sailor folk are just a daft set and dinna ken the right value o' siller. Na, na, ye'll have just made a mistake," he continued, visibly brightening at his own suggestion : " na doubt but ye mean five hundred, and that maybe would be mair nor it would be worth from a strict mercantile point of view," he concluded thoughtfully, fearing lest he might be influenced by the scriptural parallel above mentioned and be offering too much.

" Well, well, replied the sailor with a laugh and a mischievous look in his eye, " suppose we say five hundred, what then ? "

" Well, maybe," replied Ebenezer, cautiously, " ye'll be wanting siller soon, and perchance I might be able to raise as much, though"—groaning deeply—" its a tarr'ble large amount and no easy got together."

" Ay," he continued, almost bitterly, as he perceived no special sign of delight at the offer in his companion's face, " you sailors are just a reckless race and have absolutely no idee o' the value o' siller. Why, there's plenty men could keep themselves in board and lodgin' the rest o' their lives on five hundred pounds laid out at a decent rate o' interest."

His companion's ideas on the subject differed probably ; at all events, he did not immediately reply, and the two men sat watching each other in silence—Ebenezer debating within himself whether he could offer guineas instead of pounds, and the sailor mischievously pondering a scheme whereby he might outwit his host, teach him a moral lesson in the matter of covetousness, and yet retain the pearl notwithstanding.

" Well," the sailor broke out at last, with a jolly laugh, " I'll tell ye what. We'll have a carouse for the pearl. I'm not particular anxious to sell, but I've no objection to give ye a chance to get it. Look ye, now, we'll have a friendly carouse by way of a match for it—my pearl and your brass for the stakes, and grog the weapon."

" Ay, ay," he continued, laughing, " I challenge ye and
I choose the weapons. All fair and square ; you stake
your brass and I my pearl, side by side on the table, then
glass and glass about to prove which is the better man—
chalking up the score, I for ye and ye for me, as we
turn about. Then, gradually, I calculate, one of us will
feel the ship rollin' and staggerin', and will seek seclusion,
maybe, under the table, whiles t'other, still keeping right
end up'urds, wins the match, and pockets pearl and brass.

" The one that's beat can't say nothin' against it next
mornin', mind, though like enough he won't remember
much what's happened. No, no, he'll be occupied enough,
I calculate," concluded the sailor, with a hearty laugh,
and a mischievous glance at his companion, " in
refrigeratin' his headpiece as though t'were a perishable
article a-passing through the Tropic of Capricorn."

Ebenezer sat there rigid and stiff, scarce believing he
could have heard aright.

Eh ! How Providence favoured the elect ! This was
the thought that predominated in the tumultuous eddy of
his brain. Here was opportunity literally thrust upon him,
and he remembered with pride certain bouts of former
days, wherein he had gained a reputation, though he had
long since found it convenient as an Elder of the Kirk to
put away the memory of such misdeeds.

He almost felt the pearl in his grasp ; and as for the
£500, why, there it was still comfortably housed in his
trousers' pocket.

" It—it will be whisky ? " he queried hoarsely, after the
short pause wherein he had endeavoured to collect his
thoughts and maintain to outward appearance his usual
composure, " ye'll ha' no objection to the whisky ? "

"Ay, ay—whisky, for it makes one feel so frisky,"
replied the roystering mariner, not bethinking himself that
as a Scotchman his host, however reverend, was probably
acclimatised to that beverage. " Whisky, first course,
hot ; second course, whisky ; third course, whisky ; then a
brew of punch, and something tasty to eat atween whiles."
Then he broke off into a jolly laugh, and began to sing in
a full deep voice a stave or two of a drinking song.

> The anchor's **slipt** and the freight's unshipt,
>   Sing **ho** for **Jack** ashore !
> **Now** gold **doth** chink and the glasses clink,
>   Sing **ho for** mirth galore.

> The fire burns bright, Jacks heart is light,
>   Sing ho, the night arouse !
> We'll drink about till Sol be out,
>   Sing ho for a carouse.

" Whist, man, whist," exclaimed Ebenezer anxiously,
for he had now had time to reassume the mantle of the elder
which had so nearly fallen from his shoulders in the
excitement of the last few moments. " Ye canna com-
prehend the delicate nature of a good repute," he continued,
by way of explanation. " It just clings about a man like
a sweet savour, and if once suspeecion, wi' it's foul breath,
comes nigh it, it's just altogether overpowered—like
ointment o' the apothecary that stinketh by reason o' the
dead flies in it. There's aye plenty reprobates gangin'
up and down like roarin' lions seekin' to do the godly a
damage. I should na wonder," he continued, suddenly
descending to the particular, " if there were ane o' them at
this meenit wi' his lug fast to the window." With this he
stepped towards it, and lifting up the sash peered cautiously
out into the night. After he had duly satisfied himself on
this point, he closed the window, drew the curtains
carefully to, and, facing the sailor, commenced again.

" Ay, ay,"—with a sorrowful wag of the head—" there
wad be mony not ower guid themsell wad be only too glad
to bring a discredit on anither, wha wad shoot out the lip
wi' scorn and whet there tongue like a sword, rejoicin' the
while at the thought o' bringin' a scandal on the Kirk, if
ance they heard tell there had been a ' carouse,' as ye ca'
it, in the house of Ebenezer Stallybrass.

" Ay," he continued, with a sigh, after a pause, " and
doubtless there wad be some found to believe them. But
I ken a way," he continued, brightening up at the
thought, " we'll defeat them. We'll just carry up the
necessary supplies ourselves to a little bit room I ha' up i'
the garrets. It's full wi' lumber and things, but we'll ha'
a fire, and it'll no be bad. Ay, and ye can sing a song if
ye like—none will hear ye up there. I'm thinkin'," he

continued, after a moment's hesitation, " we'd better begin early while there's noises in the streets, and suspicion will no be so likely to be snuffin' about wi' her nose as keen's a game dog's. What d'ye say to nine ? "

" Ay, nine will suit me, mate," replied the sailor somewhat disconsolately, not altogether liking the way in which his suggestion had been caught up and positively taken out of his hands by his host. Indeed, he had gleefully promised himself an upholding of hands, protestations, and a ludicrous exhibition of shifts on the part of the elder in the event of his accepting this dissolute challenge and the consequent necessity he would be under of reconciling therewith his austere piety.

Instead of this, however, here was Ebenezer calmly arranging the details of the carouse as though it were a meeting of the Synod of his Kirk to discuss lay matters. He could scarcely understand it, and indeed began to feel doubtful whether he had not been premature in making the suggestion.

It was too late to go back now, however, and they parted for the night, after having agreed to take up the necessary supplies the following afternoon when the servants would be out and suspicion would not be incurred.

Ebenezer, as he went upstairs, exulted in his heart at the thought of his enemy's discomfiture ; the trap the enemy had prepared for another would be the means of the enemy's own downfall ; Providence had favoured him indeed, and he sang a song of triumph in his heart at the thought of victory. At the moment he might be compared, perhaps, to one of the grim heroes of his own church in times past, who, proud in their election, found Providence a willing ally, and justification easy, in any adventure they might be engaged upon against the person of the ungodly.

On the other hand, the sailor could not look upon the carouse that had just been planned in the same pleasing light as before until he had partaken of a stiff glass of grog ; then, indeed, he could once more agreeably perceive the elder lolling in his seat, half seas over, strugglin' in his utterance with the sanctimonious polysyllables he could

G

no longer effectually pronounce, and, delightful thought, oblivious of the fact that he had lost his "siller" and yet not won the pearl.   Enraptured by these various thoughts, both combatants sought their respective couches at an early hour.

The next afternoon Ebenezer occupied himself upstairs in the lumber room on various excuses, arranging details for the evening's entertainment, and coming downstairs now and again for the supplies the sailor surreptitiously introduced into the house.

At last the fated hour struck—the hour anxiously awaited by both host and lodger through the long interval of the day.

The host, indeed, had previously prepared himself for the carouse by a big meal partaken of at one of the Quay-side restaurants, for, as he sagely reflected, " whisky was unco' ill on an empty stammick."

His lodger, on the other hand, had purposely taken little or no food, in order to do himself full justice, as he thought, in the evening.

Punctually at the last stroke of the clock he made his way up the narrow wooden staircase that led to the chamber in the attics.   Pushing his way through the trapdoor at the top of the staircase, he emerged into a small encumbered room which was brightly lit up by a big fire, in front of which he perceived his host already standing.

The table was spread with the various weapons of the duel ; a big stone bottle, evidently containing whisky, flanked one end of the table, while a·sturdy broad-bottomed flask, that suggested rum, stood on guard opposite ; in the middle a big punch-bowl serenely rested — a noble advertisement of the coming struggle, while round about were basins containing sugar and lemons that gleamed brightly in the light of the lamp.   A slate was propped against the punch·bowl, on which stood the score to be kept by the respective combatants, each for the other, as aforesaid.   Then there were two or three side dishes containing viands of an appetising description, which were merely meant to whet the appetite for the liquor on which, as we know, the issue depended.

A kettle hissed merrily on the fire, and the sailor, as he viewed the suggestive scene before him, felt enraptured once again with his plot, and gloried in the thought of the instant duel.

" Capital," he cried, " capital, it could not have been done better, mate," and he commenced rubbing his hands briskly in keen anticipation, and hummed to himself a stave of song.

" Ha' ye brought the pearl wi' ye ? " inquired the Elder anxiously, indifferent to compliments.

" Ay, ay, here she is," replied the sailor, producing it from his pocket.

The Elder took the case carefully into his hands, opened it, and reassured himself that it was still therein, then gently placed it in front of the punch-bowl in the middle of the table. Having done this, he turned to the chimney-piece and lifted down a canvas bag which he carefully placed alongside the pearl, after having just untied the string round its mouth, and thereby exposed its golden contents.

" We'll leave them there," said he, for he felt that with the stakes before his eyes victory was doubly assured.

The combatants now sat down, Ebenezer at the top of the table as host, with the sailor on his left hand.

" The fire burns bright, Jack's heart is light," sang the enraptured sailor, grasping the stone jar near him with both hands.

Had a third person been present, he would have greatly marvelled, doubtless, at the strange scene before him, and the strangeness of the surroundings.

Here was one reveller gay and happy, flourishing his glass aloft and singing snatches of quaint ditties, while the other sat still and almost silent with a hard and constrained look in his eyes.

Then the garret in which they were holding their carouse was encumbered with such a curiously diverse sort of furniture—in one corner was a big sideboard supported by carved oak dragons, in another were carpet-bags and Chinese jars— effects of various impecunious lodgers, while on the rafters and cross-beams that bore up the low roof was piled a heavy net, though for what purpose it was there was certainly not manifest. The cord ends hung down not far above the heads of the carousers, but had not apparently been noticed by either of them.

The trap door had been shut down, and no one disturbed or was cognisant of this secret revelry, save only the parrot, who had accompanied his master into the room, and was now safely ensconced on the top of a kitchen clock in the corner, where he sat solemnly blinking at the fire, regardless of the revellers.

Meanwhile, of the two combatants, the sailor had very soon outstripped his host, who had been paying more attention to the viands, and was two glasses of grog behindhand.

But, while the latter sat steady and upright in his chair, the sailor lolled about and showed signs of an excessive hilarity, proposing and seconding and drinking the healths of individuals whose names he frequently was unable to remember, and all the time poking fun at " Old Snuffles," as he familiarly termed his host.

Now it was time that the punch should be brewed, and when he had mixed and tasted the beverage and found it inimitable, he filled his glass and proclaimed the health of " the prettiest maid in North Quay." The Elder's glass had been filled too, but curiously enough on this occasion he did not raise his glass as he previously had done in response to his companion's lead, but sitting back in his chair lightly grasped the full tumbler, watching intently, like a cat about to spring, his companion's action. A gurgling noise proclaimed the delicious draught to be ended, and the smack of the lips that followed eminently suggested an *encore*. Slowly the unsuspicious sailor raised his head—his mind wholly intent upon his desire—and just at the very moment that his eyes appeared upon the horizon of the punch-bowl, a blinding splash of spirit met them full in front. The sailor, stupefied and bewildered at the sudden attack, sat motionless for a second ; down came a thick net upon him over head and shoulders, and he felt himself fast in the grasp of the Elder.

It was not a fair fight; for the Elder, like the *retiarius* of old, had his victim fast in the meshes of the net, and soon had twined the folds round and round his arms so securely that resistance was impossible.

Then, bearing him backwards to the ground, the Elder, after having first thrust a handkerchief into his victim's mouth, proceeded to tie his legs together, and make fast and sure the knots about his chest and arms.

Seated astride his prostrate lodger, and grimly engaged upon these final touches, the joy of triumph welled up within his soul, and overflowing, found a vent in song.

" Aha, aha ! " chanted the Elder, in sing-song fervent tones, "the ungodly man thought to triumph, and like a vain fool had lifted up his horn on high, but suddenly was he dashed down and caught in the net he had laid for another."

" Ay, ay," he continued, as a sudden movement of the prostrate body underneath him accentuated the position ; "dashed down and trodden under foot is he ; and strapped tight wi' a weel-knotted rope."

The Elder would probably have continued to illustrate the paraphrase, had not the glint of the pearl, as it lay on the table, caught his eye ; hastily rising, he stepped to the table, took up his prize of victory with reverent hand, then carefully buttoned it into an inner pocket. The canvas bag he then proceeded to tie up, having done which he deposited that also in another of his capacious pockets. Then, looking about him and reflecting for a few seconds, he advanced to the window, looked out, and thus soliloquised :

" Ay, it's early yet ; may be it will be half an hour yet afore they're here. I'd just better slip round and hurry them on." So saying, he turned towards the door and unlocked it, but on a sudden turned back, and stalking up to where his victim lay, pronounced the following epitaph over him :

" Ye're no but a great fule—possessin' neither the head to carouse, nor the wut to keep yer ain."

These scathing words were finally driven home by a contemptuous kick ; then the door shut softly, a creak jarred on the stair, and the unfortunate sailor was left alone in the silent room to reflect upon the truth of the portrait.

The shock of the encounter, and the perilous condition in which he was, had effectually sobered him. Crimping apparently awaited him, to judge by the words he had overheard, and the terrible lot that was to fall on him was the result of his own pride and the poor desire to have the laugh of his sanctimonious host. Could folly herself have devised so contemptible a plot—have perilled so much for so trivial a triumph ?

The unfortunate captive groaned in spirit as he saw pass by him in fancy the various events, like links in a chain, that had led up to this final catastrophe.

Then, after having lashed himself with regrets, he became calmer, took his bearings, and finding himself lost in the breakers, resigned himself to his fate.

He saw himself carried away, a common sailor on board a vile merchant brig sent out to sea to be scuttled, the owners gaining the insurance, and no tales told.

Meanwhile Mogib, the parrot, perceiving that the noise and consequent danger, as she was well aware, had passed away, took advantage of this opportunity to fly down from her perch and settle on the table to inspect the viands and liquor, of which she had a peculiar knowledge.

Seated on a plate, she was discussing, with one eye shut, head well thrown back, and critical tongue, the flavour of the rum punch that had so pleased her master's palate.

It so chanced, however, that an unconscious movement of the captive jarred suddenly against the table leg. Mogib, startled, lost her balance and fell backwards, screaming loudly "man overboard," and bearing with her to the ground at the same time plate, fork, and knife.

The noise and clatter startled the sailor in his turn, and rolling over on his side, he dimly perceived Mogib, fragments of china, and lastly, with a sudden leap of hope, what seemed a knife close beside him on the floor.

Scarce could he believe his eyes—Mogib had then brought him this chance of deliverance! There was not a moment to be lost, for 'twould be a hard task enough to set himself free under any circumstances; and then there was the possibility of Ebenezer's returning at any minute.

Rolling over till he felt the knife underneath him, he endeavoured to gradually work his fingers through the meshes in order to get hold of the handle.

His hands being fast tied at the wrists, and his arms and chest being tightly encircled by the cord, the only possible way to set himself free was to get the knife between his hands, thrust the handle into the grip of his knees, and then, by a gradual friction of the blade against the binding of the wrists, to sever the cord.

Painfully and with difficulty his fingers pulled them-selves through the meshes, dragging the knife after them ; every now and again the blade would slip from their feeble grasp, or catch fast in some of the thick meshes of the net.

After a long and desperate struggle, during which he had several times given up all hope, and sank back exhausted from the struggle, he finally succeeded in getting firmly into the palms of his hands the trusty weapon with which he was to work out his safety. He lay there still a moment, happy but breathless, for hope had blazed up again and fired determination, and now he felt indeed his freedom was assured.

Turning over on his back, he raised his knees, thrust the handle of the knife between them, then slowly inserting the point between the cord-lappings that bound his wrists, endeavoured to cut through the strands by a gentle rubbing against the knife blade.

It was a terrible strain, and one that could not last long, for, crippled as he was, and in danger moreover of suffocation, he found the greatest difficulty in keeping all his forces concentrated upon the delicate task before him—every detail of which, indeed, as it depended upon a measurement the result of touch and not of sight, was liable to miscalculation, in which case the chance of liberty would be lost.

Suddenly there came a loosening of the cord just at the very moment when his knees had released their grip and the knife had fallen between them. Could it be that a strand could really have **parted**? With **wrist** against wrist he stretched to **the** utmost the cords; now he felt them slipping, **and then** all at once his arms were free.

A moment **before** and all **his** strength had ebbed away, but now, on a full tide, it **came** rushing back.

Seizing the knife, he **rapidly** cut through the net a **passage for his arm;** then, **this** done, sawed through the **cords that bound his chest, and in** a few **more** seconds had **actually regained his liberty.**

Now, the **question was, what would** be the **best plan of action—escape** seemed the first thing to be aimed at— revenge **could** conveniently **follow.**

The **door,** however, **proved,** on being tried, **to be** locked, and **the window, on** close inspection, was found to be too great **a height** above the ground to be available, nor was there **any projection or** pipe by which descent would have been **rendered possible.**

Well, there **was no help for it, the sailor** soliloquised; **he must just await Ebenezer's return.** To do so, indeed, **jumped better with his inclination.**

It **was certain that Ebenezer would** be back soon, but **whether he would come alone was the** question to which **no answer could be given, and yet it** was on this that all **depended.**

On **reflection, however, it** appeared probable **that** he **would return alone—his dread** of scandal would be one **reason for so doing—and then the** long rope with hook attached, **which he had discovered** fastened to the cord ends **about** his chest, **had revealed** the **fact** that he was to be lowered out of the **window into** the **arms** of the gang, who, as he had overheard, were shortly expected.

Thus thinking, he formed his plan: the door **was** locked, as we have seen, but **as** it opened **into** the room on the left-hand side, it **would,** if pushed **back** to its limit, **naturally come against the heavy** sideboard that stood behind it, and thus would **form a** place of ambush for **an assailant.** First, however, **before** taking up his position, he made up **a bundle of rags,** and laid them carefully together in the same spot where he had himself just been, dropped his handkerchief **on** the edge **of the** bundle to represent the position of the head, next strewing over it the several pieces of the net, he gathered up the remaining coils into his hands and turned down the lamp.

Then, mounting on the sideboard, he cautiously crouched on the edge nearest the door, net in hand, scarcely daring to draw breath lest the sound should betray him—all his thought suspended in revenge.

Ah! if he could once feel the Elder writhing in the meshes, how lightly would he esteem the loss of his pearl! Some ten minutes passed slowly, during which his ear, like a timid sentinel, challenged the silence and caught the fancied footfall of a foe.

Then came a creak of heavy footsteps on the staircase just below him, a slight sensation was instantly perceptible in the woodwork of the wall, a key grated in the lock, and in another moment Ebenezer's head cautiously appeared beyond the edge of the door.

Satisfied in the dim light that all was as he had left it, he stepped inside, unconscious of his peril ; at that moment, however, there came a suspicious noise from behind, but before he could look round a net fell upon his head and shoulders, and a heavy body followed instantly and bore him to the floor.

The Elder, knowing instinctively that his enemy was upon him, and no quarter would be granted, yelled like a wild beast when suddenly stricken, and fought with delirious fury. He was underneath, however, and the net entangled his movements, while the sailor, strong in his lust of revenge, with both hands had a firm grasp of his opponent's throat.

It was not, indeed, until Ebenezer's face had assumed a black and unnatural hue that the sailor relaxed his hold, and even then it was only for the purpose of binding the hands and feet of his victim tightly together.

This being safely accomplished, he could search the pockets of the unconscious Ebenezer for his pearl, not without some fears, however, for the money had disappeared and possibly the pearl had been secreted also.

But, no! there it was lying securely in its little case in a high vest pocket, and when taken out, seemed to shine with even additional lustre, as though recognising its true owner.

The tension of the last few minutes now loosened its grasp, and triumph found a voice and sang along his brain. Looking down upon his prostrate foe, his fancy depicted an instant picture of Ebenezer on board the dirty merchantman destined for himself, forced to grope his trembling way up the unused shrouds in fear of his life, rope's-ended like a cabin boy for every blunder, and finally—he who had been but yesterday an elder and edifier of the kirk—the butt and scoff to-day of godless men.

He chuckled inwardly at the delicious picture thus presented to him, but whilst he gazed, a slight stirring of the prostrate body warned him that the Elder was returning to consciousness. Taking up, then, the remains of the net, he finally completed the fastenings, and now attached the hook and chain to the bundle as they had previously been fastened to his own person.

Ebenezer had now indeed fully recovered consciousness, and struggled madly with his bonds, to the mighty joy of his secure enemy, whose eye grew mirthfuller at every fresh token of his impotent wrath.

The remembrance of the words the Elder had spoken over him when he was in the like desperate case, and which so nearly had been his epitaph, recurred to him and suggested retaliation. With a chuckle he knelt down, and in fair imitation of the Elder's slow and nasal tones, whispered impressively in his ear—"Ye're just a fool, Ebenezer, with all your self-conceit—but, mind ye a sea voyage is a splendid cure for the self-conceit, as ye'll find—ye carousin', wicked old elder that ye are!" concluded he, in his normal tones, as the wrath of the natural man got the better of the moralist.

He likewise enforced his epigram by a hearty and contemptuous kick upon the person of the Elder, which had the curious effect of immediately checking his convulsive struggles.

The tumultuous thoughts that surged up into the Elder's brain as he just recovered consciousness—the loss of the pearl, his present perilous condition, the chances of escape—had doubtless been disquieting enough; but it was the kick—the cruel indignity of the kick—that exasperated him almost to madness. The abysm of misfortune in which he lay was thus revealed to him; he could have screamed with rage had not the handkerchief been stuffed too deep into his mouth; as it was, he palpitated with murderous wrath.

At this moment, however, there came a sharp " hist " from outside, startling the sailor from his pleasing reverie, and at the same time clearly intimating to the Elder what fate awaited him.

The sailor at once cautiously proceeded to the window, and peering out, perceived three or four figures waiting in the street below. " Are ye ready ? " queried the sailor softly, imitating the Elder's voice, for he guessed rightly that they were waiting there for himself.

" Ay, ay, lower away. Sharp's the word ! " came back the answer in gruff undertones that seemed to bode ill for the comfort of the Elder, as the sailor thought with mischievous glee.

Carefully lifting up the prostrate form of the enemy, the sailor carried it to the window, and, after a brief struggle, forced the shapeless bundle through the somewhat narrow space, using perhaps rather more force than was absolutely necessary to effect his purpose.

This accomplished, he gradually paid out the rope, at the other end of which Ebenezer was helplessly swinging, till he felt a sudden stoppage; then the rope swung light and loose in his hands, and he knew his enemy was safely in the hands of the hirelings below.

Looking out, he perceived them plainly enough, making off at all speed, and carrying as best they could, their unwieldy burden.

The Elder was safely caught in his own net this time, thought the sailor, chuckling at the remembrance of the Elder in his hour of victory, and wondering whether the spiritual parallels in which he had so delighted would be able to afford him consolation in his hour of misfortune. Well enough did the sailor know that no excuses would avail the wretched man on board ship—no attempts to

prove that he was the wrong man would go down when a
ship was sailing shorthanded. No, no; there he was
aboard a dirty merchant brig, in as sorry a plight as could
well be imagined, and all, as the sailor gleefully reflected,
through his own wicked devices.

.   .   .   .

Some two or three months after the events just recorded,
had any inhabitant of North Quay been passing through
the pretty village of Moreton-in-the-Wolds, and had
inquired—been smitten with thirst after the constant
fashion of his native town—as to the whereabouts of the
best alehouse in the place, he would certainly have been
told to seek for his solace at the sign of " The Pearl."

As he proceeded thither, he would first perceive on his
approach a ponderous signboard swinging over the
entrance, on which were depicted two warriors engaged in
a desperate duel, while two armies in the background
breathlessly awaited the result. On the forefinger of the
fiercer and rougher of the two opponents was a huge ring,
which was set with so gigantic a pearl that the wearer
must have been seriously incommoded by it in the violent
struggle in which he was engaged.

Having gazed upon this stirring scene, and unconsciously
wondered what the history that was evidently attached to
it could be, he would discover, on arrival at the bar, none
other in mine host but the famous sailor—the possessor of
the wondrous pearl—who had been so well-known a figure
in North Quay for a short time some months ago, and had
outwitted the Elder in the famous episode of the carouse.

The honest sailor, indeed, had departed very shortly
after his victory, but not before he had related to his
comrades the manner in which he had got the better of the
Elder, whose strange disappearance, of course, had set
everybody speculating as to the cause.

The humour of the situation and the retribution that
had befallen the Elder tickled everyone's fancy, and
delighted many who had doubtless often been rebuked by
him for their backslidings.

The sailor, however, early escaped from attentions that

were beginning to become wearisome by a sudden departure. He had determined to sell the pearl at its own true value, and having done so, to settle down in his old home on the land belonging to the young squire, whose lovely wife, as we have heard above, he had been instrumental in helping to win.

He bought with the proceeds of the wonderful pearl the village inn, and was now fast becoming, after the squire and his wife, the most popular person in the district.

The story of the jewel had, of course, become famous, and often would mine host be pressed to tell the tale of how first it was won in fair fight against the invader ; then, how he had received it as his prize for helping to carry off the "mistress," and lastly—best of all—how he had regained it from the grasp of the sanctimonious but perfidious Elder.

DAFT WILLIE.

"DAFT WILLIE," as the village folk called him, was my constant companion during a brief stay, one "long vacation," at Watersmouth, a picturesque village on the North East coast, some thirty miles from the Border town of Berwick. Save that he was extremely sensitive, being absolutely unable to endure pain himself or witness its effect on others, and that he loathed the sight of a printed page (wherein he had my sympathy), I never was able to discover that he was in any other way inferior to the majority of his fellow creatures. He knew much more than many twice his age, though it was not of the "book larned" order, and many a long afternoon was pleasantly wiled away, as I listened to some curious narrative or other told in simplest and most direct language, and enlivened by quaint metaphor.

The following story was told to me one still September afternoon, as we lay idly on the beach together, some miles away from the village, and every now and again, at some stray touch of memory, the whole scene—the story itself and its setting—comes back to my mind in all its vividness.

"D'ye see yon twe points?" said Willie, nodding at two peaks of rock that broke the quiet surface of the water three hundred yards out at sea. "Yons the Lover's Rock, as they call it—ay, an' a tarr'ble story hangs roond it, I'se war'nt ye. There's few that's ivvor waalked the eorth that's seen a warse sight than Aa saw one neet bettor nor six or seven yeors back this month. Aa wes oot about eliven o'clock, eftor supper time, for Aa cudn't sleep, an' thought Aa might mebbies chance te spy a few ducks flyin' aboot an' feedin' on the rocks theor," pointing to the extent of rock close by on our left, which seemed to have been broken away from the cliff above under press of the waves at some former period. "Ay, theor was Aa lyin' on the bank top—in a little neuk o' rock, like a rat in's hole, spyin' a' things but nowt spyin' him, when sudden Aa heard a noise o' folks talkin', an' cranin' ower the rock's neck Aa spied the teacher an' Postmistress' daughter laughin' an' carryin' on tegither. Eh, Aa wes

tarr'ble feared seein' them theor oot sae late, an carelessly
daffin' 'on as tho' theor weor nowt else i' the world but
jist them alyen ; ay, 'bonnie Lillie ' as she wes called,
havin' had her sweetheart lang syne, an' bein' but a Sunday
or twe aff the banns bein' called i' the Chorch wi' Joe, wor
mason an' 'moorgrieve.' Theor had been words, as Aa
kna'ad, between Lillie an' Joe, an' Aa minded hoo a day or
twe agone Aa had been stannin' at the street top wi' the
Schoolmaster when Joe, her sweetheart, had passed by.
Theor she stood makin' believe she did not see him wiv her
heid i' the air, like a dog sniffin', an' laughin' loud at every
word the teacher lad was sayin' ; he was nobbut a lad still,
scarce bettor nor three an' twinty, wiv a bit hair on's lip
he wes that proud of he nivvor let go haud on't. He'd no
been i' the village lang, an' had fa'en i' love wi' Lillie at
ance ; an' Aa kna'ad weel enough he wes in love wi'
' bonnie Lillie,' an' hoo he'd written poetry aboot her,
which times he read te me. He was aye kind te me,"
continued Willie, breaking off with a sob, " an' larned me
the most o' what I hev in ma heid the noo. Ay, an' the
poetry wes aal aboot the sea, an' the sky, but it nivvor
ended wiv owt but Lillie. She wes the chorus or his
sang, an' the chorus wes aye the bonniest pairt o't.

Noo Lill te ma mind, tho' theor's some hev their doots
about the mattor, wes really i' love wi' Joe, an' Joe wi'
her, but theor hevin' been a bit quarrel both weor vexed
wi' th' ither, sae Lill had ta'en up wi' Schoolmaster te
vex Joe likely, an' Schoolmaster he takes it a' in eornest,
Aa'm thinkin', an' nivvor gies a thought te Joe, an mebbies
jist hevin' new come te the village knaa'd nowt about Joe's
sweetheartin'. Mebbies, too, he didna care ower much, as he
wes a tarr'ble passionate chap, quick an' fiery, rufflin' at a
touch ; ony way when Aa see'd Lill an' him tegither Aa
kna'ad theor was a tarr'ble danger aheid if Joe should
find them tegither, for Joe was a hard man an' was feared
a bit i' the village ; if he sets his eyes on a thing he aye
went straight for't, divvn't ye knaa, an' when he waalked
down the street folks made way for'm wivvout knaaing they
did sae, but aal folks respected him for he was a gran'
worker, an' had nivvor been seen i' liquor, even at the week
end, like most o' the cheps i 'the village. Lill must hev'

been vext wi' Joe for not takin' enough notis of her carryin' on wi' the Schoolmaster, or mebbies the Schoolmaster had been readin' his poetry te her, for she seemed a bit reckless, an' her laugh wes far louder nor ordinair', an' Aa could hear it weel from ma hidin' place i' the rocks.

Schoolmaster, he wes bendin' doon a bit to leuk intiv her eyes, an' sayin' somethin' in rale eornest, for her laugh stopped short on a sudden, an' she shrank a bit back from him. Weel, jist at that moment roon the corner th' ither side o' the rocks, who should come but Joe, stridin' alang hastily as tho' he had a purpose in 's mind. He stoppit short, an' Lill gave a sort o' start an' a bit scream, an' then stood still like a styen, while Schoolmaster he made one step back an' stood theor glow'rin' at Joe out o' his eyes an' sayin' nowt, but Aa cud see his cheek wes white as a bit paper, an' his han's were shakin' a wee. Joe, he did nor speak either but took a stride forward an' seized School-master in his arms. Theor was jist a passionate cry, an' a moment's strugglin', an then both were doon i' the sand tegither, Joe uppermost. Schoolmaster struggled ne more, an' lay theor quiet, his white face gleamin' an' workin' wi' passion—then Joe turns him on 's back, bends his arms backward, an' holdin' them tegither in 's one hand, ties a handkerchief round them wi' th' other.

Suddenly Schoolmaster raises hissel fre the sand, an' commences a fearfu' strugglin', like a beast iv a trap, an' tries te turn round an' wrench his han's free, but 'twes ne use, Joe held him like a baby, an' wivvout sayin' onythin' gies a final knot, then seizes his legs, an' binds them tee wiv a bit cord he has in 's pocket. It dis not tyek lang, an' aal the while Lill says nowt, but gazes at the twe strugglin' like one iv a dream.

Then Joe rises, silent as ivvor, an' hads awa round the rock again, an' aal is silence save a sob, as if frae a wounded beast, frae the Schoolmaster as he lies helpless, his face i' the sand.

Aa cud not move as much as a handstir, Aa kna'ad somethin' awfu' wes te happen, an' could but bide till it came.

It was nor lang for theor round the side o' the rocks came sounds of a boat gratin' on the beach, then a noise of oars workin', an' round the rocks end Aa could spy the boat

i' the moonleet, an' Joe rowin' fast wi' lang steady pulls.
Round the corner he comes, an' up he drives his craft on
the beach. Oot he jumps, an' still sayin' nowt, catches
haud o' Schoolmaster an' drops him inte the stern, like a
bundle o' rags, an' Schoolmaster cries oot in a voice Aa
scarcely kna'ad for his'n, shrill as a tern at the start, then
doon intiv a sob at th' end. "Fight me like a man," he
says, "let me free, an' not strangle me like the coward
ye are." But Joe did'na answer; he jist beckons to Lill an'
says "get in," an' Lill tyeks one look at him, myeks as tho'
te speak, but dis not, then jumps in an sits down, her face
covered wiv her han's. Joe, he shoves off, leaps in, an'
straight he shapes for the rock oot yonder.

What was his purpose Aa cud not even a guess. Aa felt
dizzy, an' scarce kna'ad what things weor happenin' tho'
theor they weor before ma eyes. Noo he's reached the
rock, an' pulls oot the Schoolmaster an' leaves him on the
rock, then he signs te Lill te jump oot, an' sae she does.
Then tyin' the boat te the rocks, he throws hissel' inte the
wattor, an' half swimmin', half waalkin' myeks for the shore.
Lill calls oot "Joe, Joe," then as he takes ne nottis flings
herself on te the rock while Joe comes plashin' thro' the sea
towards the shore. The rocks mebbies was ne mair nor
sixty yards frae the shore at the time but the tide wes
makin' tarr'ble fast an' he'd no hev won te the shore a
moment later. Gie'n hissel a shake up he comes te jist
below wheor Aa wes crouchin' amang the rocks above;
doon he sits, drippin' wi' wet, an' bides quietly i' the
shadow, gazin' upo' the rock.

T'wes a tarr'ble thing te see Joe sittin' theor, still as a
styen, gazin' at the twe figures on the rock, while the tide
wes makin' fast, an' ne'er a sound above the wattor but
the boat scrapin' agen the rock edge. 'Twes like a dream
te me leukin' on unseen i' ma cranny, an' aal ghos' like an'
unreal. Theor wes Schoolmaster lyin' motionless on the
rock, an' Lill stannin' up straight an still i' the moonleet;
Joe bidin' quiet i' the shadow below me as tho' 'twere jist
a play-actin', an' nowt te dee but leuk on contentedly,
while aal the time his sweetheart wes but a hair's breadth
frae death itsel'. What was Joe wantin'? He cud not
wish ta droon them else he'd no hev left them the boat, an'

H

yet he sat watchin' an' watchin', an' makin' ne move tho'
the tide kept makin' faster an' faster.

An' noo Aa spied one o' the figures movin' on the rock,
'twes Schoolmaster—Aa cud knaa him i' the moonleet—
who'd worked hissel free frae the tyin' an' noo wes
stannin' upright on the rock ; he leuked aboot, mebbies te
see if Joe wes onywheres nigh still, an' shook his fists
towards the land, tho' he could nivvor hev seen Joe frae
wheor he wes, then he turns an' lifts up Lill who wes lyin'
on the rock.   He kept pointin' te the boat, an' Aa cud see
him seize her hand an' seem' te drag her towards it.   But
she tyuk ne heed ov him—jist gazin' straight in front ov
her.   Aa cud nor tell what wes in her mind, but Aa'm
thinkin' she wes dootin' Joe 'd ivvor care for her agyen, an'
wes groon careless ov her life thinkin' o't.

As for Schoolmaster he wes wild like, he would hev
ta'en her awa', an' made as tho' te lift her inte the boat,
but she 'd none ov him, an' drove him awa', an' springin'
up pushed him back frae her as though she would strike
him.   Jist then Aa notticed the boat swing off frae the rock,
carried awa' by a big wave that cam' near up te the top o'
the rock.   Joe, he sees it tee, an' up he leaps an offs wi's
coat an' shoes, an in te the wattor agen tho' this time he
mun swim, for 'tis se much deeper nor before.   Straight
he strikes oot, not for the rock, but for the boat that wes
driftin' awa' north on a strong runnin' current, an' when
he reaches her, an' clambers in, 'twas mebbies some
hunner an fifty yards aff the rocks.   Whiles he wes
swimmin' eftor the boat it cam' in te ma heid that what he
was eftor wes te find oot if Lill loved the Schoolmaster or
no, an' between whiles te larn her a lesson, for Joe was a
tarr'ble proud chep an' did not dee things like ither folk.
Noo if Lill an' Schoolmaster had been sweethearts iv
earnest she would hev helped him aff wi' the cord, an'
wud hev been glad enough te get inte the boat wiv him,
an' row te land, for neither kna'ad but what Joe had
ganned right awa' lang syne.   He'd no meant te droon
them, 'twes easy te see that, an' noo that he was i' the boat
he pulled awa' like a madman te the rock which the waves
wes a'most coverin' noo.   Aa cud yet spy the twe figures
on the rock, Lill aboot two feet above the Schoolmaster,
seemin' te stan' on a ledge by hersel'.   An' Schoolmaster,

he wes turned awa' frae Lill, as tho' despairin' like noo
that she'd shown se plainly she cared nowt for 'm—theor
he wes, stannin' quite still tho' the wattor wes plashin' up
tiv his knees, wiv his eyes fixed firm on the boat speedin'
nearer. Then jist when Joe wes a'most sixty yards nigh
the rock, sudden Aa saw the Schoolmaster turn roond, catch
haud o' Lill an' seize her in 's arms, an' wiv a shout o'
triumph he flings hissel an' her inte the sea. Aa cud not
breathe i' the horror o' the thing upon me, ma heid went
roond an' roond, an' aal things were misty. Theor wes a
tarr'ble cry frae Lill as she fell into the wattor, "Joe, Joe!"
she called, an' then aal wes still as death. Aa rubbed ma
eyes thinkin' mebbies 'twes a dream, but theor wes Joe
rowin' like mad te the spot. Aa thought Aa saw for a
moment twe white faces upturned te the moonleet, naethin'
more nor that, an' aal was gyen : an' Joe Aa cud see him
rowin' roond an' roond the rock, then springin' up, mad like,
an' gazin' everywheor ower the wattor, but nivvor a sight o'
Lill. Then he dives frae the rock an' swims aboot as tho'
he maun find her somewheor, then climbs back inte the
boat agyen, an' rows te the shore, an' searches theor as if
he maun find her if he but searched lang enough.

Aa cud not bide nae mair, but fled awa' hame nivvor
restin' till Aa got back an' could tell ma granny; mebbe else
Aa had gyen clean, aaltegither, daft that neet. Sometimes
the noo Aa wyek o' neets wiv a cry i' ma ears, an' Aa see it
ower again jist as plain before ma eyes as ivvor it wes that
neet, but Aa tell granny and that mebbe helps it te pass oot
o' ma mind.

"Ah," he ended with a sob, "puir Lill, she wes that
beautiful she shud not hev deid, an the puir Schoolmaster he
wes mad wi's misery, likelies, when he kna'ad Lill had been
makin' a fyule o'm—ay, an' mebbies 'twes the deil that
tempted him, for he'd ivvor a kind heart tho' tarr'ble
passionate.

Ay, 'twas a tarr'ble neet's wark, Lill an' Schoolmaster
deid, an' Joe's good as deid ; 'twes said he drifted out te
sea in 's boat, an' wes picked up by a vessel, an' that he
listed in foreign parts ; onyway we've nivvor seen nor
heord o'm again. 'Twes a tarr'ble neet's wark—an' aal, as
one may say, because ov a bit o' pride."

BY BUDLE BAY.

ON a certain November night, long remembered in that part of the country, some thirty years ago, a fierce Nor'easter was raging all along the harsh coast of Northumberland. The storm had sprung up suddenly, as is not unusual in that region, but a careful observer from certain premonitory signs might easily have foretold its coming.

All afternoon the cattle had been drawing closer to the lee side of the dykes for shelter; many a plump of sea fowl had been speeding inland off the sea; the drooping clouds to the eastward had lost their separate shape, and were merged in a single, heavy, and opaque mass on an ever nearer horizon.

As the afternoon wore on, the fisher-women drew closer and closer to the fire-side, thanking God their men were not out at sea that day, and the wild-fowler, watching the in-drawing of the sea fowl, had taken down his fowling-piece from the rafters, and was furbishing it up, rejoicing in the prospect of to-morrow's sport.

Towards sun-down, jets of white spray might have been seen playing against the basalt cliffs of the inner Farnes; the "megstone," or Cormorant island, had long since disappeared from view, while afar to the southward Dunstanbro's "churn" was sounding, in prelude to the battle.

As evening drew swiftly on, hugh wave furrows, deep driven by the wind plough, crashed continuously upon the strand. The air smoked with salty mist; the gale thundered aloft, as though with claps of mighty sails, and well the little group of watchers on Budle sands knew that the big ship they had marked that afternoon, labouring deep in the rising sea, was helpless as a new-born babe that night.

Still, however, they waited on, in hopes they might be able to rescue some poor shipwrecked soul who might chance to be washed up ashore. Her minute guns had ceased to sound, and once, when the gloom lifted a little, they had spied her fast amidst the breakers, pooped time after time by mountainous waves.

Rockets had been fired unavailingly ; indeed, against the stress of storm it scarce seemed possible to carry so far, and in the prevailing mist 'twas hardly possible to more than vaguely guess her whereabouts. Suddenly, however, one of the keenest sighted amongst them became conscious of what seemed a black smudge upon the churning breakers nearer shore, a trembling spot of darkness that now soared upward for a moment, and then was lost to view amidst the foaming ruin. The eyes of the entire group were instantly turned in this direction, and all stood breathless, peering forth with strained eye-balls, to discover whether fancy had deceived their comrade, or whether it might not chance to be a human form. A simultaneous cry escaped the lips of the watchers, who had insensibly drawn down to the margin of the waves, for there on the surface of a mighty billow hung for a moment an evident patch, outlined against a curving edge of foam. There it hung an instant, but whether a spar from the wreck or a human form could not be known, for it sank immediately from sight into the seething cauldron below. Yet once again, and nearer shore the black patch rose and peeped amidst the surge, and at the sight the strongest of the watching group plunged boldly forward, a rope about his waist, into the blinding waves. Soon he had fought his way till he was close beside the object of his search, then as he stooped to grasp it the ebb sucked back the helpless bundle from his hold, and tossed it like a ball to the following wave that, deftly catching it, swung it aloft in triumph, and hurled itself upon the pigmy figure below. Yet the figure, undaunted, stretched out his arms to catch the falling object ; the wave broke over him, and nought was seen upon the hissing surface.

The group on shore tug bravely, running backward as they haul, for the weight is heavy, and the ebb is eager for its plaything. Yet now the strand is reached, and the group breaks up and rushes down to seize the black object lying motionless upon the sand. Fast in the arms of his rescuer, himself insensible, the limp and drooping figure of a sailor is discovered, a life-buoy gripping him close beneath the armpits, sore battered by the waves, to all appearance lifeless.

Lifting up the two dripping bodies they carefully bore them up the beach and over the sandy dunes to where, in a hollow, stood a small house, sheltered from the winds. This house was the home of the fisherman who had so gallantly rescued the shipwrecked man, and served also as a small ale-house or refreshment tavern in the summer for the wayfarer who might be travelling to the island beyond. The slim form of a girl came timidly through the darkness at the approach of the company, anxiously inquiring what had kept them so long.

Kindly the rough men, bidding her be of good heart, informed her of the rescue, and calmed her fears for her father's safety, telling her a drop of brandy would soon put him to rights, though as for t'other, 'twas more than doubtful if he was not already beyond their aid. With quick understanding she at once sought out the necessary appliances, carried blankets to the fire-side, and drew forth from a recess a flagon of brandy, which one and all pronounced to be " tarr'ble canny for the livin', and the best thing in the waarld for drooned men." Quickly they undressed the two men, and, disregarding the advice of the eldest of the group who insisted upon their temporary suspension by the heels from the rafters, swathed them in hot flannels and laid them down by the fireside, some chafing the numbed limbs, and others endeavouring to force hot brandy down their throats. They succeeded in getting some down the throat of their comrade, but found it impossible in the case of the stranger to secure the passage of the restorative. "Ay, poor chep, I doot he's gyen," said one, after a last fruitless endeavour, and this being the universal opinion they forsook a hopeless task, and sipping at the steaming glasses their hostess handed them, patiently awaited the course of events. Some minutes passed away in silence, then suddenly, to her great joy, Nell (for so the girl was called), saw signs of returning life in her father's countenance; a faint colour had come back to his cheeks, his lips trembled, and he heaved a sigh; in another moment he had opened his eyes, and with a struggle raised himself with the help of her outstretched arms, to a sitting posture on the floor.

"A'm reet enough, thank-ye ma lass," he said, "an' thank ye te, mates, for what ye've dyen, but hoo's the poor chep." To the astonishment of the group he stopped dead short in his utterance, his eyes fixed at a stare upon the face of the lifeless figure on the floor. Then his lips moved, and they heard him mutter to himself "Black Jim!" Leaning forward from where he sat he pointed to the right ear of the unconscious sailor, and at once the silent group about him, following the line of his pointed finger, perceived that the lobe was wanting.

"Ay," they further heard him mutter to himself, "'tis he, shure enough, there's nivvor another like him i' the waarld."

Curiously enough, and as though the presence of one evidently well known to him in the past had penetrated to his consciousness, the figure of the shipwrecked man now gave signs of a return to life. The eyelids were seen to twitch, and a slight and uneasy motion passed through his body.

The assembled group, dumb with astonishment at the strange turn matters had taken, looked uneasily, first at their companion sitting swathed in blankets by the fireside, and then at the stranger lying pale and deathlike on the floor beside him, and felt that there was something most unchancy in it all. To think that these two were old acquaintance, and should have chanced together in such guise, yet that Straughan should care no more about his chance of recovery than if he had been a drowned kitten. "Ay, 'twas tarr'ble strange, and no just canny." Such thoughts passed slowly through their minds, and all sat silent till Nell gave voice to the universal curiosity, when, recovering from her astonishment, she asked her father: "Ye'll never have been knowin' him, father?" "Ay, I knaa'd him weel lang syne," responded he, looking straight before him into the fire, "ay, an 'twas little gude I knaa'd of him cither."

Pondering inwardly upon this strange meeting, and
perplexed as to what could have been the relationship
between their old comrade and this unknown stranger
whose destiny yet hung in the balance, the rest of the party
continued silently to chafe the limbs of the shipwrecked
sailor, but with increased hope now that life was evidently
still fluttering within. They were so far successful, indeed,
that soon his pulse could be felt to beat, though so feebly
that only Nell, with her delicate fingers, could be sure that
it was really at work again. But now at last they con-
trived to force some brandy down his throat, and this
accomplished, it was felt that the corner had been turned.
His eyes were still fast closed, though some mutterings
escaped his lips, and the general feeling now being that
Nature should be left to work out the further cure they
lifted up the unconscious stranger from the floor and laid
him in the four-post bed in the corner. Meanwhile their
host, worn out by his exertions, or possibly overcome by
hidden emotion, lay in fitful slumber on the floor, and him
they raised in turn and lifted on to a rough settle by the
ingle nook, securing his comfort as best they could.

Nell was now persuaded to go upstairs to her room and
take some rest, her kind friends assuring her they would
look after her father and see that he wanted for nothing.
The door closed upon her slight form, and they were left
alone, and now at last their tongues were free to wag upon
the strange event of the night.

The creeping and delicious sense of mystery indeed had
suddenly entered into their life, than which there is to
mortal man no chiefer savour in the world.

Straughan, indeed, though an Islander by birth like
themselves, had early run away to sea, and on his return
after many years had always been tongue-tied about the
past, and had been on this account credited with a strange
and adventurous career. To have their suspicions thus
almost verified—to have romance actually brought to their
very door cheek was as treasure trove to these home-keep-
ing men, who still looked upon railways as an " uncanny "
mode of travel and a " fair temptin' o' Providence." " 'Tis
a fearful strange thing, this, lads," said the eldest of the

group, a grizzled, weather-worn fisher, the leading Methody
and local preacher on the island, "a fearful strange thing,
though maybe heor as elsewheor 'tis the hand of Heaven
workin'." "Ay, 'tis a strange thing, sure enough, an'
maybe 'tis Providence an' maybe 'tis no'—'tis a matter
beyond our knowin' an' useless to spekilate upon," said
another and younger man, the well-to-do publican of the
"Fisherman's Rest" on the island, who, having quarrelled
with the "priest" on the temperance question, had
seceded from church, and, scorning chapel, had set up
for himself as a "nattoril Christian" in the matter of
religion, and was wont to sustain his position on occasion
by a battering of received theology—"but what'd be better
worth knowing, and 'tis a proper matter for consideration,"
he continued, "is what for Straughan leuked se evilly on
the poor drooned chep of a furriner theor. He was weel
acquainted with him for he acknowledged that hissel, but
he bears him an ill-will, 'tis plain as dayleet, an'
Straughan's a gey canny man, as canny as ony that ivor
waalked the eorth, an' no one to mislike a man unless he'd
a proper call; ay, it mun hev been a mighty big thing to
put Straughan agen him like that." The conversation
having thus been given the right practical turn, all specu-
lated concerning the supposed cause of Straughan's enmity
against the stranger, and finally, after various theories had
been started and rejected the scales hung even between its
being a woman or a buried treasure. Eventually the
woman theory, backed by the local preacher, triumphed
over the treasure theory which the "nattoril Christian"
had found it necessary to uphold.

"Ye see," quoth the victorious Methody, by way of
clinching the argument, "ivor since the tyem of the garden
of Eden a woman's been consarned in aal the mysteries of
the warld, an' 'tis no like that this tyem she should be left
oot—an' did ye no' mark the furriner's fyece? 'Twas a
sinfu' fyece yon, an' one that likelies be ivor nosin' aboot
eftor women like a gyem dog eftor partridge; I'm no ane
to hammer a man wivvoot a cause, but natur's natur, an'
'tis only a fyul will run his heid agen a plain like wall."

A murmur of assent ran round the circle, and a grave

nodding of heads ratified the conclusion. Scarcely had
these sounds subsided, when the figure on the settle moved
from its recumbent posture, rose to its feet and walked to
the bed whereon the stranger still lay unconscious. To the
surprise, and possibly a little to the disappointment of the
others, Straughan seemed suddenly to have changed his
bearing towards him, for having felt his feeble pulse he
turned and spoke in altered tones: "It'll maybies gan
hard wiv him, mates, he'll likely hev had some bones
broken in aal that buffetin', one of ye'll maybies gan for a
doctor whiles we dee the best we can till then."

One of the group of fishermen immediately volunteered
to undertake this commission, and as the gale was now
subsiding as rapidly as it had arisen, and grey morning
was flickering in the east, the rest of the company rose to
depart to their several homes.

It was some time before the doctor arrived, and in the
meantime the patient had awoke to consciousness and discovered himself to be in possession of all his faculties and
apparently uninjured by his terrible experiences, though in
a very weak and battered condition. His recognition of
his rescuer and former companion, Straughan, and the
various emotions, on either side, that accompanied it,
were matter of speculation amongst the curious, but none
ever knew what had transpired, for it had taken place
before the doctor's arrival, and Nell had been absent from
the house at the time.

No bones were broken, the physician reported, and no
internal hurt had apparently been sustained, but rest and
quiet were enjoined, and a fortnight or more must elapse
before the patient could with safety set out again upon his
travels. Many were the visits of inquiry, serving as a veil
to curiosity, that the islanders paid to the house, but it
was little they learnt for their pains. Straughan was more
reserved than usual, and seemed to take but little notice of
his guest, who, however, appeared to be very much at his
ease, carrying himself, indeed, throughout these visits in so
arrogant a manner, and with such a tyrannical pretension
that one and all gradually came to the conclusion he was
a pirate, and wondered if Straughan would not be for

"shifting" him. The stranger, however, in these inter-
views, never let fall anything from his lips that threw any
light on his past relations with his host, so that this, even
after a week had passed, was still matter for acute conjecture.

Nell, however, with a woman's instinct, quickened,
moreover, by filial love, had divined from the first that in
some mysterious way the stranger possessed an influence
over her father. It was evident, too, to her (and this it
was that rendered the matter tangled past all unravelling),
that her father actually feared this same stranger. 'Twas
strange, indeed, that he whom she had thought nothing in
the world could ever gliff should be afraid of anyone.
Why, it was her father who had alone dared to withstand
that fiery-head, the blacksmith, when he was roaring
drunk, and had sworn to kill his wife.

Now from this dread there seemed to follow unavoidably
the inference (though she sprang ever from it as though it
were a defilement) that her father had committed some
crime in the past, and that this stranger knew of it. She
did not believe it for a moment, and yet, and yet it seemed
as if it must be so, for her father did not interfere, though
shortly after their guest began to pay attention to her, nay,
even to court her. He frightened her, so she could not
resist him as she would, and ever and anon, when she
would not answer him, he would let fall some hint or
cunning suggestion of the evil case her father stood in did
he, the stranger, wag but a finger. Hotly she disregarded
these suggestions, yet the sight of her father's altered
countenance could not but strengthen them, and often-
times she noted that he could but barely conceal the fire
that quivered in his eye, or shut in the words that trembled
on his lip when Black Jim talked with her of an evening.
Sometimes he would even rise and go out, pacing up and
down outside for an hour, when he would return, the passion
gone from his face, but in its stead a pained and harassed
expression never seen there before.

Daily the unwelcome stranger, as he grew stronger,
grew bolder, pressing his suit the more as the time for his
departure drew nearer. Despite a natural aversion to the

man, Nell could not but feel there was a certain attraction
about him ; throughout **his** very braggadocio, carried to
the verge of recklessness, **there** breathed an evident air of
mastery ; he **smelt of** battle, **as it were,** and his easy
speech was fragrant with memories of victory. The
champion wrestler at the fair, in the hour of his triumph,
she minded, had had an identical gait.

To her he ever deferred, however arrogant with others ;
his stories of adventure she could not but listen to, so rich
in excitements were they. . He had seen the wonders of the
world and had brought back chips of them, as it were, in
his pocket.

As her **aversion to him** died down, so her fear **of** him
increased ; **everything, it** seemed, he had ever set his hand
to had so prospered **that one** might believe Providence herself had stood gossip to him at his **birth.** That heavy
underlip of his **what purpose and greed** of power it
revealed ! And when she saw those bold eyes of his fixed
upon her, their prominent whites shining brightly beneath
his dark and bushy eyebrows, she felt her knees tremble
under her and her power of resistance vanish in thin air.
She had ventured to approach the subject with her father
on one or two occasions, and had timidly enquired as to his
former acquaintance with their guest, but had ever been
vaguely answered and comforted by the assurance that the
stranger would soon depart, and there an end of the
matter.

There wanted now but two days to the date of his
departure when her father, calling her aside early in the
morning, intimated that he had arranged for her to spend
the next two days at her aunts on the Island, and not to
return until Black Jim should have gone. " Ay, lassie,"
he said, " I'm loth to let ye gan, you an me that's nivvor
been parted syne the neet Heaven gave ye to me, but 'tis
better sae, for Black Jim's worse than a deevil, an' I
could'na bide ye bein' i' the hoose wiv him any longer. To
see him coortin' ye, or makin' a pretence o't, as it likelies
is, an' me prevented frae thrustin' him to the door, why, to
burn in hell would be mair pleasin' nor that." " Ay,
lassie," he continued, sorrowfully, as he gave her a final

kiss, " he's got a bit hold on me, that's the truth, but he'll
be awa' in two days, an aal ull gan reet wiv us then. I
canna tell ye the reasons o' things now, but ye'll nivvor be
dootin' yer fayther, whativvor happens, will ye lassie ? " he
cried in conclusion.

Protesting truly that she had never for a moment entertained a single unworthy thought of him, and that her
anxiety was solely on his behalf, she endeavoured to
assume, notwithstanding a sense of impending calamity, an
appearance of light-heartedness she certainly did not feel.

After this conversation with her father, Nell went
at once to spend the two days before the departure
of their unwelcome guest, at her aunt's house on the
Island, in order to be out of the way of any further attentions on the part of the stranger. Late in the afternoon of
the next day, which was also the day before that fixed for
Black Jim's departure, Nell determined that she would go
across the water to see her father once again ; she knew
she was in this disobeying his wishes, but a strange rest-
lessness had tormented her all the morning, she had slept
ill and her dreams had been full of a fear of some impending misfortune, so that it was with a feeling of relief that
she finally set off for her father's house.

On arriving there she found that the door was locked,
and concluding her father and his guest were out was
about to turn back sadly, when she heard the sound of
voices raised in dispute from within. Stealing round to
the little low window at the side of the house she saw
through a crack in the shutters three figures within, two of
them gesticulating as though in anger. One was her
father, the other " Black Jim," and the third, a dark-
skinned, evil eyed foreigner, evidently a sailor from his
appearance. Terrified at the sight she stood still, unable
to move a limb, then catching the mention of her own
name she became aware that the window was not fast shut,
so that by kneeling on the ground she might be able,
unseen, to discover the meaning of the mysterious drama
now toward within. Swiftly she knelt on the ground,
applying her ear to the minute opening above, and found
she could catch, for the voices were raised in dispute and
the night quiet, the conversation carried on within.

" Ay, that's my ultimatum," said Black Jim, " so make your choice ; 'tis the gallows awaits ye if ye don't agree." " 'Twas ye that killed him, an' Mingo and I'll be ready to davy it at the 'Sizes, blowin' the trouble of it when 'tis for the sake o' justice, won't we Mingo, my hearty ? " turning maliciously towards the foreigner as he spoke. " Ay, ay, Mr. Jim, for the sakes of justice, ha, ha, berry good, berry good ! " re-echoed his companion, showing his teeth in venomous laughter. " In confidence," continued the first speaker, " and between us three that knows the facts of the case I'll acknowledge 'twas a disappointment to me that the coin came down tails and singled ye out for the job, for 'twas a matter of knifing to save the lives of all, and him the cowardliest brute ever I sailed under, but in a court of law, why, 'tis another matter, an' with all them lyin' lawyers about 'tis enough to deflect the very compass itself, an' Mingo an' I would likely enough be found swearing we'd tried to prevent ye from doing it, but ye were ower quick for us." " Berry good, berry good," interrupted the stranger, again smacking his lips over the last few words, and repeating them over to himself while the other continued. " An' what'll be the result of the trial ? why I'll tell ye for certain what it'll be." Pausing, he left it blank, but an ugly motion with his hand round his gullet and a throwing upwards of the whites of his eyes plainly signified what that blank would be. " Ay, ye were aye unlucky, Straughan, an' that's a fact, 'twas aye heads with me an' tails we ye, an' now ye are in the tightest place ever ye found yourself in in your life, an' ull have to haul down the flag, an' quickly too. Mingo an' I have got ye at last, after twenty years seekin' for ye, and savin' up our revenge in the hope of finding ye at home some day, and now, an' now "—The speaker here broke inconclusive off, rubbed his hands swiftly together, drew in his breath between his teeth, and glanced triumphantly at Mingo, with such a fire of hate burning in his eyes that the poor girl looking on, dropped momentarily to the ground in terror. " Never yet," he went on, " did I take a blow from a man without paying him back the double of it, and here's this

d——d scar of yourn," touching as he spoke a jagged line
that showed immediately below his cheek bone, "been
yelping at me daily ever since that day we parted for its
repayment, an' Mingo here, whenever he chaws his food
most naturally curses ye 'twixt his mouthfuls." Mingo
smiled evilly, nodding in affirmation, and disclosed a black
gap in the ivory line of his teeth. "Ay, Straughan, no
doubt ye thought ye were extraordinary clever that day
when ye choused me as ye did, but ye'll not be thinkin'
yourself so clever to-day, perhaps," he added with a sneer.
"Ay, ye choused me of a fine lass that afternoon, but now
ye've got to make it up to me with another, and her your
own. 'Twas a downright foolish, as well as an
ungentlemanly trick ye played chousing your old mate out
of the bonny Indian lass, an' never to gain any good
yourself by it—ay, an now ye've to pay a two-fold debt—
first, for the lass, an' second, for this mark of your cursed
fist."

He paused for a moment, and then continued in quieter
tones, which only served however (as the poor listener at
the window thought to herself), to throw into greater relief
the black hate of the speaker's heart within. "But I'm
willing to deny myself a bit, for I don't forget that t'was
ye who pulled me out of the sea t'other night, not but
what any one of those stout fellows there might have done
the trick instead, but bein' as 'twas, I say I'm ready to
make matters pleasant for ye if ye don't set up any further
foolishness. I'll not force her to say yes by tellin' tales
against ye until I've up an' axed her to take me on my
own account, not but what she must have made a shrewd
guess ye're in my power, for she's quick is the lass, an'
ye've been behaving ever since I came feet foremost into
the house like a gaol-bird in presence of a beak. If she
says no, why then let the law take its course, says I, for
I'm for law, an' order, an' security, an' the use o' steel for
carvin' o' mutton only, like any trembling cit o' them all
now I'm for settlin' down as long-shore man. But mind
ye, she'll say yes, don't be feared, for she's taken to me
uncommon, an' small blame to her either, says I. An'
what a selfish chap ye are, too, thinking only of yorself all

the while, an' never of her at all. "An what d'ye think
would be her feelin's when all the world was pokin' the
finger of scorn at her for bein' the daughter o' a gallows-
bird, as so they will if ye don't strike sail to me. 'Tis a
handsome offer I'm makin' ye under the circumstances, yet
here ye are sulky as a bear, sayin' nothin' to it all; why
'tis no manners at all ye've got!" he cried, tauntingly, for
his victim still sat silent, his head averted as though he
scarce listened. His right hand, however, stole unconsciously towards his left hip and groped in search of a
weapon, then, finding nothing, fell helplessly back to his
side again, and at that Black Jim, who had mockingly
watched the movement, burst into a laugh and taunted
him afresh.

"Ay, ay, mate, but ye're not aboard ship now, remember, an' ye'd best not play any of those tricks with us, or
'twill be the worse for ye." And now at last Straughan
broke his long silence. Facing round he showed a
countenance wherein, save for his eyes that glowed like
lamps, was not a particle of colour, and thus burst forth:
"Hell yawns for ye, ye black-hearted scoundrel, ay, an'
I'll pay ye what I canna dee myself; 'tis just the thought
of her, an' what her misery ud be that keeps my hands
frae your throat, an' keeps ye safe till your time comes.
Ay, but I pray Heaven it may be soon—an' maybies
Heaven ull hearken to a poor man's cry that never, save
once, an' that alone for the sake of others, has soiled his
soul wiv guilt." These last words were pronounced in so
low a tone that it was doubtful if his two companions
caught them, but Nell, outside, whose ears were at their
keenest stretch, heard, and could scarce restrain her
anguish.

There was a space of silence for a moment, broken only
by the sound of Black Jim's mocking laugh, then
Straughan, who seemed suddenly to have repented of his
outbreak, made a fierce attempt to control his passion, and
after sundry hesitations stumblingly commenced in a
changed and apologetic tone: "Maybies I'm ower hasty
in the temper yet, ay, an ne doot I was selfish, for 'tis her
I've to think about an' no mysel', an' maybies it'll be best

for me to give in an' haul down the flag as ye wor sayin'
wivout more ado." And he sank back in his chair like
one defeated, his face wearing a blank expression, the
flame dead in his eyes. "And now," he continued, and
there was such apparent cheerfulness in his voice that the
pale watcher outside was herself almost deceived, "we'll
myek an end of threats an' such like, an' hev a proper
unnerstandin' about the matter. Ye say ye'll use ne
compulsion, an' if Nell says "aye " ye'll marry her sure an'
fast—byganes 'ull be byganes, an' aal will be reet. An
dootless she'll give you "aye " as ye were thinkin', for 'tis
hard for a woman to say nay to a chep like yersel' that
gans about wiv his pockets clinkin' wiv brass." " Ay,
mate," replied Black Jim, upon whom the flattery was not
lost, " now ye're talkin' sense, an' as ye've climbed down
I'll be ready to make things go as pleasantly as can be.
But, mind ye, there's to be no shilly-shally here, else ye
might be slippin' through our fingers again, an twenty
years of waitin' be thrown away. I'll off this night an'
seek out Nell an' get my permit, as I think 'twill be. If
so, an' 'tis "aye," then we'll off to-morrow to Edinburgh an'
be spliced there that very afternoon, for Edinburgh's
where I'm settlin' doon, an' Scotland's a fine place for
matrimony on a sudden. Do ye agree mate ? " he asked
abruptly, dropping his jovial tone and assuming again a
threatening expression.

"Ay, I'll agree, say no more on't," replied Straughan.
"Well then," continued the other, content with his
acquiescence, " we'll allow ye to come and see the last o'
your daughter, but the moment the knot's tied we part
company, an' off ye sheer for good an' all. An' mind ye,
ye're not to attempt to see her till I've had my say, nor
any ways till to-morrow, when ye'll be able to congratulate
her on the good choice she's made. An' now, Mingo, my
lad, now that all's ship shape, lets have a carouse, an'
then I'll away to the island to pay my respecs' to the
missus." So saying, he turned aside to the dresser, where
stood sundry bottles, and with Mingo's help at once
commenced his preparations.

Meanwhile, Nell, outside, was strengthening herself in

I

the determination she had arrived at whilst listening to the conversation within. It had needed all her power of self control not to force her way in and take part with her father in the cruel struggle that had been going on within. Now she was glad of it, for prudence told her she had acted wisely. Yes, she had made up her mind and would act at once. Never would she allow her father, whom she passionately loved, to become the sport of their revenge. There was but one way to save him from their cruelty, and that way she would take. Ay, would she, ay, and even marry that fiend within, though marriage with such as he was a thing to spit upon. Then, having married him, the next day she would find a way to fly from him, would re-join her father, and they two would flee together somewhither, to some corner of the earth beyond Black Jim's kenning.

Ah, why had her father not trusted her love? Why had he not told her about all that had happened in the past? There was nothing that could turn away her love from him, and 'twas a brave deed, too, he had done, even Black Jim had granted that. 'Twas his love for her that held him back from telling her, fearing she might look askance at him, doubtless; oh, but the pity o't, for 'twas now too late, and Black Jim, with revenge burning in that black heart of his, had him tight in his keeping. Never mind, she would outwit him yet, for a woman's wits were sharper than a man's, as she'd often heard tell. Doubtless her father thought she would refuse Black Jim, but she would not. Ay, that was what he was thinkin' on when he agreed to the scheme, hopin' to gain time and circumvent his enemy in the end. There was not much time to lose however, for she must be back at the island to collect her thoughts and have her answer ready. One last long look at the little room within, which but yesterday she could have confidently said she would never leave while life lasted, but which she now felt certain she would never see again. So she looked long through the hole in the shutter, and in below the sash, and noted the quaint but beloved objects belonging to what henceforth would be a former existence.

There were her father's long sea-boots and oil-skin petticoat hanging from the heavy beams ; there on a nail above the dresser his sou'-wester, while in the corner lay the "squills" with the long lines she had often helped him to bait of an evening, a pleasant three hours' task as they chatted together sitting opposite one another on their "crackets" with the mussel-filled pail between them ; then above the dresser, too, lay one by one the many curious articles she had often laughed at him for keeping, not that he wanted them, but had simply bought to propitiate " lang nebbed Nanie" the uncanny pedlar woman with the evil eye, the fear and dread of all the fishermen, who was always to be found by the beach when the cobles put off of a morning. Ay, there they all were, and she must leave them, but she would leave them gladly, for to-morrow she would save her father, rejoining him never to part again. One last loving look at him as he sat there in his chair, brooding and haggard, to keep up her own strength for the sacrifice awaiting her, then she must fly, for time was pressing. A sigh escaped her as she gazed for the last time upon the humble room, then with firm lips she turned swiftly away towards the island.

She had been back there not much above an hour when there came a sudden knock on the door, and instinctively she knew that " Black Jim " was without. Going to the door herself she opened it and met the sailor face to face. " Why, 'tis the fair maid herself," said he with an air of boisterous gallantry, "that's fortunate, for 'tis with yourself and not with auntie I'm anxious for a talk. Can ye step outside for a minute, my lassie, and hear what I've to say ? " She nodded assent, and closing the door quietly, followed him down the little street to a space of open ground where they could speak without attracting notice.

The sailor commenced warmly to protest his love, and assured her it was with her father's permission that he did so, then began to expatiate on the benefit to all concerned, when, to his surprise, Nell turned towards him and said, " Ay, I'm ready to marry wi' ye." It was but a momentary sensation, however, for, after all, had it not always been so with him ? had not women ever fallen plump, like ripe fruit, into his arms whenever he had jogged love's tree?

"That's a sensible lass," responded he, folding as he spoke her passive form in his arms and imprinting rough kisses on her cheek. "I thought to myself maybe she'd taken a fancy of her own free will to rough Black Jim, an' maybe ye'll be ready to marry me in a hurry like," he continued, "say, to-morrow, for your father's agreeable, an' tis best so for he's been ailin' of late, as I daresay ye've noticed, and on your account, as I know right well, and once ye're married belike there'd be a weight off his mind." "Ay, I'll be ready," quoth Nell again, impassively as before.

"Ay, an' will ye?" responded the sailor in rapture, for he had foreseen difficulty here, "Why, ye're the very identical maid for me, for your fie-fie missie hath a weary trick." "Ha', done," said Nell, firmly, escaping from his arms, "I'll marry ye, an' that's enough. Wait here a minute," she continued, imperiously, "and I'll send a message by ye to my father." Without waiting for reply she fled away, re-entered the house, and hurriedly wrote five little words to her father on a scrap of paper, enclosing a ring he had given her long ago. She then returned to the sailor, who was pacing up and down outside inclined to be wrathful at her sudden change of mood.

"Ay, she's a bit of a vixen yet," he murmured to himself, "but a week or two o' livin' with me will put that right soon enough." She thrust the paper into his hand and bade him deliver it to her father, but barely listening to his injunctions as to to-morrow's plans. Whilst he was still speaking she turned away, escaped from his embraces, and was gone. "Ye're an ill-tempered hussy after all," quoth the disappointed sailor, hotly, "but so much the better—'twill be all the sweeter revenge, ay, it'll taste all the better for a little opposition."

Opening the scrap of paper he deciphered in the dim light the following words, "All will be well, dear Father." "Aha," he chuckled to himself, "I was no' mistaken, she's a 'cute lass yon, an' smelt the danger her father was in." Tearing up the paper and thrusting the ring into his pocket he sauntered off to relate the news of his acceptance to his future father-in-law, rejoicing in the thought of a first taste of revenge, for it would be a greater triumph were he to say nothing of the message and tell Straughan she had willingly accepted him. With an inward groan (for his last hope of delay was thus shattered), Straughan heard, and took the ring. Yet perhaps after all it was but another of his devilish tricks, and he might yet find a way to outwit Black Jim at the finish. So all the evening through he sat revolving stratagems, while his unwelcome guest made merry and feasted in his house, all the while keeping a watch upon him, for he and Mingo had agreed to keep him within eyesight until their purpose was accomplished.

Slowly the night waned for these three ill-assorted companions, each busied with his several thoughts. The Lascar and Black Jim wiled away the hours with jesting and gambling, and gloated over their near revenge, yet not daring openly to voice it lest Straughan might yet, if rendered desperate, escape their clutch by some mad deed. And all the time they drank and jested at the table Straughan sat silent in his chair gazing deep into the fire, planning to outwit his enemies even in this last extremity.

Nell had sent him back the ring as token she would marry the sailor, and never a message with it. Could she really have taken a fancy to the villain after all? No, no, it was impossible, she knew of course (for he had told her), that Black Jim had a hold on him, and she thought to save him thus. Yes, that would be like her—the noble girl, but she should not do it, he would find some other way.

When at last the grey dawn trembled in the east, he rose wearily and stumbled out of doors in hopes that the fresh air of morn might provide counsel to his brain. The sailor motioned Mingo to follow him and prevent, if such were his intention, his going over to the island. An hour or more passed as Straughan roamed distractedly over the sandy dunes, savagely meditating, but only to reject, plan after plan, and all the time, as he was conscious, the figure of the Lascar stole secretly behind him like some grey shadow of approaching doom.

On one thing alone was Straughan determined, to save his darling from the sailor's grasp, for well he new what marriage meant, even if marriage was intended, with such a man. A month of petting till lust was gratified, then a thrusting forth to harlot it in the streets for a living.

Yet what could he do ? turn this way and that he could see no path of deliverance. Black Jim was not invulnerable, yet there was the Lascar to deal with also, and both, he knew, were watching, like hawks, his every movement. Were he, secretly, now to plunge himself into the waves he might escape their vengeance, but his lovely flower would still remain to be plucked by a ruthless enemy. Full of despair he stood still upon a knoll and gazed upon the waves that seemed to him to mouth in scorn at him and his helpless plight, and filled with voiceless melancholy he was tempted to "curse God and die." Yet at that very moment a sudden inspiration leapt like a ray of light into his mind, ay, there was a chance there, he thought, a wee bit of a thing but likely yet, for the sailor, like all evil men, was greedy and easily tempted. Maybe he would save her yet, and they would fly together, for they'd get a good bit start any way ; folk might think it had happened an accident, and that there was nobody in the house, and might be slow to the rescue. Quickly turning, he strode back to his house dandling his idea in his mind, turning it this way and that as he went, till he was satisfied on every point. As he neared the house, the strident voice of his enemy, raised high in exulting song, came roaring from within through the open door-way, scattering fragments of a ditty to the outer air.

> " O luck it is a fair woman
>   That halts 'twixt yea and nay,
> The lusty knave will win favour,
>   The tim'rous fool hath nay.
>
> 'Bove all, cries she, I love the man
>   That smells of the salt sea.
> Merry he is, and lief he is
>   To pay the bussing fee.

" Ay, ay, Black Jim," he murmured savagely to himself, "ye've elwis been lucky, ne doot, but maybies ye're strainin' Providence ower far the noo." Entering the house with an appearance of joviality, (for he had a part to play) he thus addressed his enemy. "Just been for a jaunt, mate, to liven me up for the day's business; but it's time now I was puttin' Nell's things into a trunk, for tis near the hour to be startin'. The machine's to be by the Beacons in half-an-hour, I believe. I'll no want anything for meself for I'll return the neet when aal's finished in Edinburgh."

"Ay, ay, that's ship shape, look slippy there, for I'd no like to keep a lassie waitin' on her weddin' day, 'tis no gentleman likes that, an' 'tis insulting to the ladies, ain't it Mingo?" said Black Jim, addressing the Lascar, who had by this time also returned. Straughan forthwith proceeded upstairs to his daughter's little room and quickly filled her trunk with her belongings, dragged it downstairs, re-entered the room where Black Jim was sitting on the top of a sea chest the Lascar had brought with him, still chanting his ode to luck.

"I'm ready for a start now," said Straughan, "there's but a thing or two I'm wantin' yet. I'll carry the trunk an' ye an Mingo can take the chest atween ye. There's just one thing I'd near forgotten," he continued, "an that's a bit dowry I've set by for Nell, ye'd best tyek it wiv ye now, for I'll no want it mysel', the fishin' an the hoose here will support a single man an' somethin' ower."

Black Jim, who had just begun to shoulder the chest, glanced suspiciously at the speaker for a moment or two before replying, but seeing no trace of ill faith in his host's manner, the devil of greed stole into his soul, for he hesitated a moment longer, then said roughly: "Where is it, is it part of the old haul? gold, or what is it?" "Ay," was the response, "there's gold in bags, an' there's bars, as were saved ower from our last voyage from Peru, ye'll find it up i' the loft there. Gan up the ladder, an' lift the door an' ye'll find yourself in a little lumber-room, there's nets an' sea-goin' matters put awa' for the winter; I'll show ye the way if ye like, 'tis hid in the far cupboard an' theor's the key," throwing it, as he spoke, upon the table. The sailor took it up slowly, again hesitated a moment or so, then turned to his host and said with a suspicious frown on his brow. " I'll go myself, alone, thank ye, an' lest ye should be at any tricks, Mingo will stay behind here an' watch ye ; mind ye, Mingo lad, keep an eye on him, an' if he's up to mischief raise a shout for me." So saying he turned towards the small ladder in the corner, while Straughan, carelessly seating himself on the table, commenced to light a pipe. The sailor ascended and disappeared, and a few moments later came mysterious sounds of heavy bags thrown upon the floor, then the rasp of metal, at which Mingo's ears pricked greedily and his lower jaw dropped expectantly. " Maybies it'll be as well for ye to gan up and help him, 'tis gay heavy is gold, 18 carat too, I'se warr'nt." 'The Lascar looked at him with quick suspicion, then listening again to the sounds upstairs greed almost conquered prudence, for Straughan's careless manner was re-assuring. Still, however, he lingered dubiously, half fearful of his ancient foe and mindful of his watch. " If yor fearin' owt, ye may bind me," said Straughan carelessly. " I'm fearin' we'll miss the train," and he held his hands out temptingly behind his back. The Lascar jumped at the offer ; whipping out of his pocket a big bandana handkerchief, he quickly tied it round and round Straughan's wrists in hard knots, then sprang to the door, locked it, put the key in his pocket, and bounded up the ladder to the loft above. " D ——ye, what d' ye want here ! " Straughan heard Jim growl as the Lascar appeared above the loft door, " down wi' ye at once an keep guard as I telled ye." " All's berry well, Mr. Jim, me's tied his hands an' locked the door," said Mingo. There was a pause, then Jim's head was thrust through the opening ; seeing Straughan sitting quietly there with his arms tied behind him, his suspicions were allayed, and with a scornful laugh he hurried back to his treasures. " Ay, he's fast enough, Mingo, an' now with your help we'll fill up this box an' carry it downstairs. There's a tidy heap here, an 'twere a sin to leave it."

A look of relief passed over Straughan's face as he still sat motionless below, listening with straining ears and parted lips to the conversation above. Then a hot glow of purpose leapt into his eyes ; yet not a moment was to be lost, the Lascar's timidity had well nigh ruined his chance. And all this while, with ears still quick to follow the progress of events above—his outstretched hands had felt and had found the chimney of the lamp which was still burning on the table, for the morning had been dark. There he stood, motionless and eager, not a muscle of his face moving a hair's breadth while the flame struggled with the knots of the handkerchief and crept along his wrists ; still not a muscle moved, though a smell of scorched flesh rose into the air. Ay, now it was giving way, thank God the charred rags had parted at last and he was free. He bent down and with his smoking hands pulled off his shoes, laid them down noiselessly, sprang across the room to the ladder and stole as lightly as a cat up the steps. Not a moment too soon, for as he clutched the ring of the trap door he caught his enemy's eye not three yards away dragging his booty to the stair. Black Jim made a spring forward, but the trap clanged heavily, grazing his heel in its descent. Shooting the heavy bolt home, Straughan descended the ladder and kicked it down, then going to a recess in the wall he drew forth a large can of oil. " Ah, there's plenty for the job," he said quietly to himself as he carried it towards the bed. Seizing the bed clothes he dragged them down, pouring the oil carefully over all. Then to the table and seizing the lamp, he broke off the chimney against the table edge and flung the lamp into the soaking mass of bedding.

Bravely the flames leapt up, jostling each his fellow in their hurry to tear and devour their delicate prey. Bravely they leapt and crackled as they spread further, while from the loft above came a roaring as of caged beasts and a trampling as of iron heels. " Ay, Black Jim," said Straughan to himself, as he listened to the turmoil above, " an', maybies ye're no singin' yer ditty to Luck the noo ; a'am thinkin' she's tired o' ye at the finish."

So saying, he moved quickly to the narrow window, which he hastily thrust open, looked anxiously out, and seeing nobody about, sat quietly down in a chair to meet his doom. Ay, he was trapped himself, Mingo had done the trick for him by locking the heavy door, the window was scarce two feet across, 'twas useless to attempt it. Ah, well, he did not mind overmuch, maybies he'd have been caught after all even had he got away for the time, and Nell was saved.

"God, maybies, will pardon me yet, offsetting my life to theirs, for I was sore beset. An' noo, sweet lassie," he continued in a louder voice, as though a listener might be present, "good-bye, an' dinna mourn ower much when a'am gyen." The fire, so quickly grown in strength, was now roaring upward to the roof; upstairs no sound was audible. Through the thick smoke that rolled along the floor, the flames stretched out lean fingers that clutched at the motionless figure in the chair. In another moment that space was empty, and a heart of flame pulsed through an empty shell of walls.

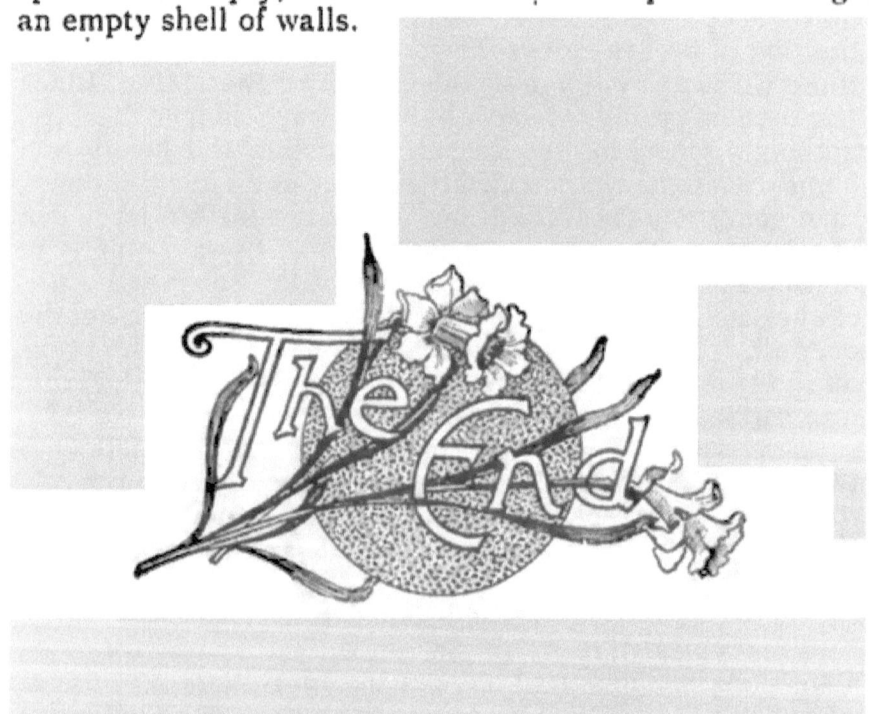

Printed by Messrs. Mawson, Swan, & Morgan, Newcastle-on-Tyne.